**They stopped kissing, but still Roman held her. Anya could feel his body was broader, more primed, and she ached, simply ached for him, for the years he had denied her his touch, his body.**

She should tell him to go. Now was her chance to do just that.

Roman knew, too, that he should leave, instead of resurrecting them.

*Once,* their eyes said.

*Just this once.*

Their bodies could kiss the other goodbye.

Without a word he went and turned the key in the door.

He was back.

For *their* closing night.

## Irresistible Russian Tycoons

*Sexy, scandalous and impossible to resist!*

Daniil, Sev, Nikolai and Roman have come a long way from the Russian orphanage they grew up in. These days, the four sexy tycoons dominate the world's stage—and are just as famed for their prowess between the sheets!

Untamed and untouched by emotion, can these ruthless men find women to redeem them?

You won't want to miss these sizzling Russians in this sensational quartet from *USA TODAY* bestselling author Carol Marinelli—available only from Harlequin Presents!

Find out where it all started in:

*The Price of His Redemption*

*The Cost of the Forbidden*

*Billionaire Without a Past*

# Carol Marinelli

## RETURN OF THE UNTAMED BILLIONAIRE

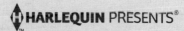

HARLEQUIN PRESENTS®

Recycling programs
for this product may
not exist in your area.

ISBN-13: 978-0-373-13441-0

Return of the Untamed Billionaire

First North American Publication 2016

Copyright © 2016 by Carol Marinelli

All rights reserved. Except for use in any review, the reproduction or utilization of this work in whole or in part in any form by any electronic, mechanical or other means, now known or hereinafter invented, including xerography, photocopying and recording, or in any information storage or retrieval system, is forbidden without the written permission of the publisher, Harlequin Enterprises Limited, 225 Duncan Mill Road, Don Mills, Ontario M3B 3K9, Canada.

This is a work of fiction. Names, characters, places and incidents are either the product of the author's imagination or are used fictitiously, and any resemblance to actual persons, living or dead, business establishments, events or locales is entirely coincidental.

This edition published by arrangement with Harlequin Books S.A.

For questions and comments about the quality of this book, please contact us at CustomerService@Harlequin.com.

® and TM are trademarks of Harlequin Enterprises Limited or its corporate affiliates. Trademarks indicated with ® are registered in the United States Patent and Trademark Office, the Canadian Intellectual Property Office and in other countries.

**Printed in U.S.A.**

**Carol Marinelli** is a Taurus, with Taurus rising, yet still thinks she is a secret Gemini. Originally from England, she now lives in Australia and is the single mother of three. Apart from her children, writing romance and the friendships forged along the way are her passion. She chooses to believe in a happy-ever-after for all and strives for that in her writing.

## Books by Carol Marinelli

### Harlequin Presents

### Irresistible Russian Tycoons

### Playboys of Sicily

### The Chatsfield

### Empire of the Sands

Visit the Author Profile page at Harlequin.com for more titles.

# CHAPTER ONE

EVERY TIME SHE danced it was for him.

It was the closing night in London of the spectacular ballet *Firebird*.

The last time she had been here, Anya had gone from being one of the princesses and an understudy to dancing the leading role.

Now, due to popular demand, the stunning ballet was back.

It was Tatania, Anya's stage persona, the gathering audience had come to see.

The theatre was packed and Anya had been told that there was a duchess in the audience tonight; yet Anya would dance only for him.

For Roman Zverev.

Her first and only love.

Apart from ballet.

The hours of practice and absolute self-control, the rigorous preparations and the endless reach for perfection Anya did for herself.

Yet, when she danced, it was *always* for him.

Now she had her own dressing-room. Like most performers, Anya was swathed in superstition and her dressing table was prepared like an altar. It was filled with tiny trinkets she had gathered over the years and specific make-up and brushes that were all neatly arranged.

She had warmed up. Her feet were bandaged and her pointe shoes had been broken in—there were other pairs ready if needed. She had already scraped her straight brown hair into a tight high bun and whitened her face. Carefully, and with great precision, she applied the black and gold make-up that enhanced her pale green eyes.

Everything was done to order.

Now, as she was given the half-hour call, she took a drink of coconut water and slowly ate half a banana. The other half of the banana she carefully wrapped and would eat during the interval, along with a small chocolate treat.

Anya loved chocolate.

It reminded her of Roman.

After she had eaten, Anya dabbed her mouth and then she put on her headpiece of red and gold feathers. She carefully secured it, checking it over and over. Happy that it was firmly in place, she painted her lips crimson and then called for the costume manager.

She slipped off her silk robe and stepped into her costume. The tight-fitting bodice was a deep red with orange and gold appliqué and the ten-layered tutu was adorned with silk feathers.

Anya raised her arms as the concealed zipper was closed. The costume fitted perfectly and showed the long slender lines of her arms and legs.

Out in the real world, her tiny frame drew stares and whispers because Anya was so very thin, and yet that tiny body was a powerhouse of lean muscle and she was incredibly fit.

Oh, every single day, she worked for it. Hours of training and rehearsal and rigorous self-control meant that her body could perform feats most others could only dream of. Yet, despite her command on the stage, right now she shivered with nerves as the ten-minute call came and the costume manager did a final check.

Now she was Tatania, her stage persona.

*'Merde!'* the costume manager said—the dance equivalent of 'Break a leg'—and Tatania nodded but did not respond because her teeth were chattering too much.

She wrapped a heavy silk shawl, one that she had bought for her mother, around her bare arms and shoulders.

Her mother, Katya, had been a single mum and a cook in a Russian orphanage. She had died recently but had lived to see her daughter reach these heights and for that Anya was grateful. Katya had had a vision for her daughter long before Anya had.

As a young girl, Anya could remember practising her dance steps in the kitchen of the *detsky dom* where Katya had worked. As Anya had grown older, rather than going home to their tiny cold, empty house, she would go to the orphanage and practise her steps with an ache of hunger in her stomach for the stew her mother cooked.

Sometimes she would sneak a taste but, if caught, her mother would give her a slap.

'Do you want to get big, like me?' Katya would say.

Of course they had clashed, though never more so than during her teenage years.

'No boys,' Katya had said, when she had caught Anya staring at Roman. 'Especially not one like Roman Zverev. He is trouble.'

'No,' Anya had said. 'He just misses his twin.'

'The twin he beat up, the twin he scarred.'

'No,' Anya had attempted, 'that was just because

Daniil refused to be adopted without his twin and it was the only way Roman could get him to leave.'

'Don't answer back,' Katya had said and had pulled down the roller blind and sent Anya to the back of the kitchen. That night, once home, Katya had spoken more harshly to her daughter. 'There can be no boys. To succeed with your ballet you can have only one focus.'

Anya had obliged—there had been no boys.

But a few years later, away from the orphanage, she had met Roman.

And he had become a man.

Ready now to take herself to the stage, Anya looked at her trinkets and touched them. She opened a small box but did not take out the bunched-up piece of foil. She would save that for the interval. Instead she ran her fingers over a faded label. It was a label that she had torn from the sheets when she and Roman had first made love and beside it was a small gold hoop earring.

Tonight she brought the label up to her lips and then replaced it back in the box and snapped the lid closed.

There was a knock at the door, and she was informed it was time. Anya made her way through the maze of corridors in the old London theatre. *'Merde,'* was said many times but still she did not respond.

Anya did not make friends readily. Her only focus had been getting to the top and they all thought her cold.

She was.

Anya was the queen of ice.

Until she danced.

Mika was there; he wore a suit of red and a small cap, which would soon hold a feather that the firebird would give to him. They nodded to each other but that was it;

they were immersed in their own pre-performance routines.

The press insisted that they were a couple. Mika had quite a reputation with women and, such was their chemistry on stage, it was assumed it carried on afterwards.

In truth they did not really get on.

Anya wasn't particularly close to anyone.

Once she had been. Until Roman had left her, there had been laughter and passion and she had been open to others.

Not any more.

The audience started to applaud and Anya shrugged off her shawl and did a final limber up as the audience hushed and the orchestra teased.

*'Merde,'* she said to Mika as he picked up his bow and arrow, the props used for the opening act, and, before her very eyes, he became Ivan, the prince, and went onto the stage—the setting for the magical garden.

Anya took some deep breaths and her teeth chattered as she fought nausea. Even after all these years, she still suffered with the most terrible stage fright and the more she advanced in her career, the worse it became.

It was an incredibly demanding role and the pressure on her was immense.

She moved several steps back and positioned herself and, closing her eyes, she took in some slow deep breaths and waited for the moment.

When it came, she was no longer Anya, or even Tatania.

As she flew onto the stage, she *was* the firebird.

A flash of gold, caught by the light, darted across the stage and she heard the audience gasp. The sight of the firebird intrigued Ivan, the prince.

Now he hid behind a tree as the firebird waited on the other side of the stage, taking more deep breaths and preparing to stun the audience again.

She did so.

Now the prince hid in the garden in wait to watch and then capture the firebird, and after another pause she came back on and swept up a piece of golden fruit.

Firebird was so beautiful, Anya thought as she danced. So slender, fragile and graceful. Few knew the agony that it took to birth this beauty and tonight, on closing night, it all came together as she shimmered and danced for him.

For Roman.

The man she had loved too much.

Their love affair that had lasted for just two short weeks but then he had so cruelly left.

For a long time she had feared he had died.

He had not.

And he had never once told her he loved her.

Had he? And would she ever see him again? Firebird asked herself over and over as the prince captured her in his arms and the *pas de deux* commenced.

There was a small flutter of hope that she might— soon the dance company would move to Paris and that was where she was now sure he lived.

Would Roman seek her out this time? Firebird wondered as the prince lifted her high into the sky.

Left alone on the stage towards the interval, she danced her solo with everything she had.

Everything, *everything*, was right.

The interval came and she did not respond to the chatter from her colleagues; instead she shut herself in her dressing-room. For the first ten minutes she just recovered her breathing. The role was the most demanding of any of them. Then Anya ate the other half of her banana and a small chocolate bar and closed her eyes, desperate to not escape the zone that she had found tonight.

And with the sweet taste of chocolate on her tongue she remembered her first taste.

Always she had practised in the kitchen, but once she had become a teenager, her mother had told her she could not dance when the boys were eating, as it teased them.

She would put on an apron and serve their meals instead.

Oh, but there was one she would love to tease.

Roman.

He and his twin had a talent for boxing and Sergio, the maintenance man, trained them and insisted that the Zverev twins would make it in the boxing world.

As a younger girl, Anya had laughed as they'd trained and had told them that she was far fitter.

She had been.

Anya had been accepted at a prestigious dance school, but in the holidays she would come back.

There were four boys, and they were always together—Roman, Daniil, Nikolai and Sev.

Trouble the workers called them.

Anya didn't think so.

But on the eve of Daniil's adoption by a rich family in England, a fight had broken out and Roman had won.

She could remember Daniil sitting in the kitchen as her mother had done what she could to repair his cheek.

'The rich family don't want ugly,' Katya had said to him as Anya had fetched the first-aid box.

She had looked at Daniil and seen the confusion in his eyes that his brother could have done this to him.

'It's because Roman wants what is best for you,' Anya

had wanted to say, for it had been clear to her that Roman had not really been cross with his brother, just let him think he could do better in boxing without him.

She had been too nervous to say that in front of her mother.

After Daniil had left for England, the little group of four had quickly disbanded.

Sev had been given a scholarship to a very good school and had later boarded there.

Nikolai had, they'd thought, run away and thrown himself in a river. But, as they had recently found out, he had simply run away.

Only Roman had remained in the orphanage.

Now, at mealtimes, Roman had come for the second sitting, the one reserved for the older, most troubled boys.

He had been so beautiful. Dark hair and pale skin and he'd had black eyes that would look across the dining room and catch Anya's at times. Always she had been aware of him and anticipated his arrival. Even on the coldest of mornings, when he'd come in to breakfast, there had been heat in her cheeks, just because he had been near.

In the evenings, when she'd served him his stew, sometimes their fingers had touched under the plate he'd held out.

Anya had lived for those moments and ached for time to speak with him properly, but he had been in the secure wing, so it had been an impossible dream. Sometimes she'd convinced herself that she was imagining that Roman felt the same way about her, until one night when their fingers had met beneath the plate. He had given her something and Anya frowned as she'd felt the slim package.

Worried that her mother would notice, she'd quickly put it into the pocket of her apron but then, when she'd been sent to the cupboard to eat her soup, she'd taken it out.

Chocolate.

Belgian chocolate.

And a whole bar!

How had he got it?

And why, instead of eating such a rare treat himself, had Roman saved it for her?

Oh, her mother had found out. She had opened the cupboard door and found Anya pushing chocolate into her mouth.

Katya had berated her daughter as she'd slapped her, but for Anya it had been worth it, not just for the sweet taste, more that Roman had thought enough of her to give her such a treat.

All these years later she still had the foil and, as she touched it, she smiled at the memory.

It was time to return to the stage.

With her mother's shawl wrapped around her, again she painted her lips scarlet and then back through the maze of corridors she went.

Firebird soared even higher.

She danced the monsters into the shadows and as she did so, she thought of the lover who had left her.

How he had broken her heart when he had left without so much as a goodbye.

But she had risen.

Anya had poured all her grief, her anger and her longing into her next love—ballet.

And it had paid off, it would seem, for she was here, under the lights, now a prima ballerina, enchanting the audience, whom she held in the palm of her hand tonight.

How the firebird mocked the monsters on stage as she danced them into exhaustion and yet her energy remained.

Just as she always did, she imagined Roman watching as the prince held her and turned her and she was perfection in his arms. She hoped Roman ached in regret for leaving her behind.

As the magical egg cracked open, she closed her mind to the grief and the memory of his smile filled her heart.

Flu had swept through the orphanage and the orphans had been confined to their dorms. Walking into his room in the secure unit to deliver his supper, just before he'd left the orphanage, they had been alone for the first time for a moment. How she had ached to lower her head and kiss that sulky mouth.

'How did you get the chocolate?' she had asked.

Roman hadn't answered but she had warmed to the first glimpse of his smile.

And tonight she was on fire to the memory of it.

But then it had been over.

Firebird did not appear in the final scene; instead she sat on the floor in the wings and dragged in air, utterly drained. Then as the performance ended, she listened to the cheers and the applause and she hauled herself up. When it was her turn, the firebird ran onto the stage as serene and as beautiful as ever to accept the applause.

The audience rose as she returned. They knew they had seen an amazing performance tonight and that she had danced with all that she had.

Tatania offered deep curtsies, swooped and picked up the roses that were thrown onto the stage.

She knew that she had earned every bravo and every cheer and Tatania smiled as still they cheered on.

There was a ten-minute standing ovation and over and over they called her back to accept the applause, but just as the noise started to ebb, she heard it.

*'Brava krasavitsa!'*

Beautiful woman.

Tatania froze momentarily and turned her face up and to the right and peered into the darkness but she could not see him.

Yet her soul recognised his voice.

Roman was here.

# CHAPTER TWO

IT WAS NOT the words that made her freeze, because there were many Russians in the audience and she heard that phrase often. No, it was the depth of his voice that made her face lift and her eyes scrutinise the darkness, and for a brief second in an otherwise faultless performance, she was Anya Ilyushin.

The cook's daughter.

The orphans had all thought her posh because she'd had a parent and had later attended a prestigious dance school where she had learnt not just to dance but to talk well and to eat and walk like a lady. They had not understood that she too had been dirt poor. Before she had boarded at dance school and later during the holidays, she had risen before five in a freezing house and had gone to the orphanage with her mother. There, unlike at home, the kitchen had been warm. Katya would work all day and through till late at night, not just cooking but cleaning and scrubbing and sorting out supplies. Once her mother had put the oats to soak, ready for the morning, they would return to their dark, cold home, ready to do it all again the next day.

Anya had always yearned for the next day. When she was there, she had always looked out for him.

And she was looking out for him now.

Now she peered into the dark of the audience, but he did not call out again. Perhaps she had misheard. Or maybe she was going mad, Anya thought as she made her way back to her dressing-room.

Now she was exhausted and aching.

She sat there at her dressing-room table and fought to concentrate as she was told that soon she would receive the duchess.

'Who else?'

There were many people who would want to greet her, and Anya found she was holding her breath as the names were read out.

Last year, when she had first played Firebird, Daniil, Roman's twin, had been in the audience and had come backstage to make sure that it really was her.

She had run to him as for a tiny second she had thought it was Roman, but even before she had seen the scar, her heart had collapsed as she had realised it was not Roman.

She was scared to get her hopes up again.

Yes, she understood that it was imperative that she greet the duchess and she gave a terse nod. Of course one of the sponsors was here and with him his teenage daughter, who wanted to be a ballet dancer too. Anya felt her hands ball in impatience as the list was read out.

'Who else?' Anya snapped.

'There is a gentleman, he says that you would remember him as Daniil Zverev's twin...'

Anya's heavily made-up lashes fluttered as it was confirmed that Roman was here, yet he had not directly given his name.

'He offered his congratulations for your performance

tonight. He said that he always knew that you would make it. He asked that I pass on this.'

Anya glanced down and there in the assistant's palm was the small, thin gold hoop that she had left behind the time they had first made love.

Oh, she remembered coming home that day, late of course. Her mother had asked where she had been.

'Your earring is missing,' Katya had said, and then she had seen her daughter's glittering eyes and flushed cheeks and her mouth and skin inflamed from Roman's rough, hot kisses and she had slapped Anya's cheek.

Hard.

And then the other.

Now Anya's cheeks reddened at the memory of their first time and the bliss that both had found, and now Roman had brought the earring back to her.

'Tell Daniil's twin that he can return it himself. You can bring him to my dressing-room *after* I have greeted the others.'

Oh, she ached to have the pair. Her mother had given her the earrings when she had been accepted into the school of dance.

But, no, it would be a cheat to her heart and it would scald her fingers to take it from anyone other than Roman.

For now she had to line up with the rest of the cast, and as the duchess congratulated her on her performance, she shivered with the hope that Roman was still near. Tatania curtsied deeply and smiled and conversed with the duchess, but her breathlessness was not from awe, but for the potential moment to come.

She greeted others that she had to and accepted their congratulations with grace. She spoke with the sponsor's young daughter and even gave her a pair of pointe shoes.

Yes, she did all the right things until finally she sat at her dressing table and told the assistant that she was ready to receive her final guest.

She stared into the mirror and saw that the feathers shook in her headdress and her eyes were wide, as if in shock.

She was.

After all these years they would come face-to-face and speak.

Oh, she had seen him once, a couple of years ago, but it had been from a distance and Anya did all she could not to think of that time.

*All* she could.

There was a knock on the door and she could not stand or turn. All she managed was to call the word *Enter* in Russian.

And still, as the door opened and then closed behind him, she did not turn.

Her skin shivered just to have him close.

He came into view in her mirror. At first there was just the darkness of his suit and the whiteness of his shirt, but it was enough to let her know that his body was still delicious. Oh, better even, because he was taller perhaps and broader, and as he came and stood behind her, Anya forced herself to look into the mirror and meet his eyes.

Roman was more beautiful than she remembered.

His hair was shorter than she recalled but was still black and glossy. The black eyes that met hers warned her heart to still fear him, for even after all these years he had the absolute power to hurt her again.

She could not recover from losing him twice.

Three times, in fact, but she chose not to go there in her mind.

It would seem that the years of despair she had suffered through had suited him. The man she looked back at was polished and poised and the cologne she now inhaled was heady.

He commanded her senses—he always had, for whether he wore cheap denim or a designer suit, the effect of Roman up close was the same.

Her senses did not point out the differences.

They did not care that the fingers that came to her shoulder were now manicured.

Just his touch had her fighting not to arch her neck, to rub her cheek against his hand.

He was back.

That was all she knew.

And as his hand remained on her shoulder, the contact had her eyes close in the ecstasy of his touch.

*'Brava,'* he said.

'Roman.' It was all her voice would allow.

For Roman, just one word was almost too much—hearing his name from her lips, the familiar slight huskiness of her voice, made locked-away memories pour in.

Finding out that his brother had married, that Daniil's wife had just had a baby, had hit Roman like a fist. Knowing that he had a niece and that his twin was now a father had been difficult and he had fought not to make contact.

He could remember a worker speaking with him on the day of the fight, the last time the four had shared a dorm. Called into the office, Roman had been nonchalant as he'd been used to being in trouble.

'Daniil is talking about not taking this opportunity unless they adopt you too.'

Roman had sat.

'They don't want you.'

Roman had said nothing.

'Do you remember when you were four and that family took you for a walk?'

'*Nyet.*'

'They were a married couple and were considering adopting the two of you, but they said you were too wild.'

Roman had vaguely recalled something of the kind. They had been taken to a park and he had remembered standing on a swing for the first and only time.

'Back then we said we would prefer not to separate twins. Roman, Daniil lost an opportunity once because of your poor behaviour. Don't let this happen again.'

'Tell him that if he goes, when I am older—'

'No.' Immediately the worker had interrupted him. 'I don't think you understand the opportunity this is. Daniil will be receiving a private education, he will be given the best chance for a new life. Do you want your twin to have to look out for you? To support you?'

Never.

'You need to do the right thing by him and let him go for good.'

And he had.

Daniil now worked in London. Roman told himself he was here to purchase a property—that it happened to coincide with *Firebird*'s return was a coincidence.

In the end he had bought a ticket for tonight's performance.

Dressed in a black suit, ready to leave his luxurious hotel, Roman had sat on the edge of his bed and stared at the earring and told himself to tear up the ticket.

To not go back.

He had made a vow to himself that he never would.

Yet he had gone to the ballet and watched silently in

a box seat. His breath had caught when Anya had first briefly appeared on the stage.

And then again.

He had watched her dance and had ached with pride for all she had achieved.

That little girl who had diligently practised over and over in the kitchen, the teenager who had devoted herself to her dream was now a prima ballerina.

And she could not have made it this far with him.

He knew that for a fact.

Standing to applaud, Roman had meant to leave then, to slip away with the precious memory of watching Anya perform at her peak, but unable to resist he had called out to her. He had watched her face lift and her eyes search for him and he admitted to himself that he had lied about slipping away, for he had brought with him the gold earring that he had found on the floor as he had cleared out his bedsit.

No, he reasoned, for he took it with him everywhere.

Would she want to see him?

Roman didn't know.

And now Anya asked a question he could not answer properly.

'Why are you here?' she said. They spoke in Russian and it had been a long time since Roman had used his native tongue, but he slipped into it with unexpected relief.

'To congratulate you, of course,' Roman said. 'You made it. I always knew that you would.'

He leant forward and Anya breathed in again the heady scent of him and felt his arm brush her bare shoulder as he placed the missing earring on her dressing table.

She picked it up and remembered them at eighteen, lost to the world, wanting only each other.

'You told me you couldn't find it.'

'I couldn't,' he said. 'But when I packed…'

He had packed everything he had into a small backpack and left without even a goodbye.

'You could have come and given it to me.'

'No,' Roman said. 'Because we would have ended up making love. It had to be that way.'

She couldn't dispute that they would have ended up making love, neither could she forgive his choice to leave, but that he had kept her earring for all these years meant so much.

Anya wanted to open the small box and put the earring with its partner but she decided to do that once he had gone. She did not want Roman to know just how much she had missed him, so she placed it back down and stood and turned to face him. She was tiny compared to his large frame. Her breathing was too shallow but face him she would, even if it nearly killed her to do so and to see all she had lost.

He looked immaculate.

His glossy black hair was superbly cut, he was beautifully clean shaven and scented with expensive cologne. His suit was exquisite, so much so that she reached up and touched the lapel. His chest was a toned wall of muscle beneath her fingers and she could feel tears pooling in her eyes as she saw a different Roman from the impoverished youth she had known.

His hand came and took hers, at first to remove it, because contact was too much, but then it closed over hers.

Now she lifted her eyes to his and they stared and the years that had parted them seemed to drift away.

No one could move her like Roman and it was the same for him.

'Where have you been?' she asked.

He did not answer when there was so much she needed to know; she could almost feel his reluctance to tell her.

'It doesn't matter.'

'It does to me.'

'I cannot stay long.' Roman shook his head yet still he held her hand.

'You could at least take me to dinner—we can talk properly. There is so much to catch up on.'

'Don't you have an after party to go to?' Roman checked. From the shadows he had watched her accept the duchess's congratulations and had heard the chatter.

Still they held hands, but now their fingers were entwining and their palms were exerting beats of pressure as the flame that had never died started to burn brightly again.

'I can miss it.'

'No.' He shook his head. 'We didn't do too well at dinner last time, remember?'

A laugh caught in her throat as she remembered the one time they had been in a restaurant together. Roman, trying to make his way as a boxer, had taken her out for a Valentine's Day dinner, using his winnings from a fight.

Valentine's Day had still been relatively new in Russia but Anya had wanted to celebrate it.

She had wanted flowers and, of course, chocolate.

Roman had taken her to a restaurant, though.

The first restaurant they had been turned away from as Roman had not had a jacket and tie, and in the other restaurant it had been just as much hell on the inside.

A menu had been handed to him, when he had never known such a thing even existed.

There had been a wine menu too.

He had wanted to give her everything, except he'd had nothing to give.

Nothing.

But he had taken care of her aching body after rehearsals and soothed her panic as she'd prepared for an important audition.

They had lain in his room and talked, they had glimpsed a future, even if Katya had said it would be an impossible one.

And then, without warning, he had gone.

'You left me…' She said it with the pain she had felt then and his hand was warm over hers as she jabbed at his chest.

'Anya, I had to. You would not be where you are today had I stayed'

'You don't know that.'

'But it's true,' Roman said. 'You wanted to get to Saint Petersburg and you did.'

'You could have come too. We could have got a flat—'

'It would never have worked, Anya. I could not afford a flat for us and neither could I sit back and say nothing about…'

He did not finish, both knew what he referred to.

Oh, their night at the restaurant had been such a disaster.

They had left and gone back to the small bedsit he'd had and it had been the blackest of Valentine's Days, Roman had lain there, knowing that he had embarrassed her with his unpolished ways.

No.

Anya had stared at the ceiling, wondering how she might excuse that three-course meal. There had been steak and *hren*, a horseradish relish that she adored, as well as wine. A large meal, though, was the very last thing she'd needed before such an important audition. She'd known he had spent everything that he'd had. Roman had thought good food would help her tomorrow. Yet it had sat on her stomach like lead and she'd known it would weigh her down.

Once she'd been sure he'd been asleep she had crept to the tiny bathroom and knelt down and done what she'd had to do to make the next day work.

Her shame when the lights had gone on she felt again now.

The row that had followed had been as passionate as they.

'What the hell are you doing to yourself?' Roman had shouted.

'You don't understand how tough the competition is.'

'Nothing is worth that! Anya, your mother is wrong to tell you...'

He never got to finish.

Embarrassed at being caught, still trying to save the situation, Anya had jumped to Katya's defence. 'She does what is best for me. Roman, you don't understand families.'

She'd regretted her choice of words so badly because Roman's eyes had shuttered.

It was the last conversation they'd had.

No, Anya thought, perhaps he could not have sat back idly as she'd done what she'd had to in order to get where she was. She had never made herself vomit since that time. Instead she controlled her portions and worked hard on her body, but few understood the discipline required.

'Where have you been?' Anya asked.

'France,' he said. 'Corsica...'

'So you did join the Foreign Legion?' She just stared at his huge hand over hers and tried to hold tears back.

'Yes.'

Anya knew about the French Foreign Legion because during their precious time together Roman had hinted that it was an option, and so when he had left she had looked into it. Legionnaires were given a new identity, passport and birth certificate.

Their pasts were wiped clean

And it meant that the soldier you loved so much might die but you would never know.

'Rather than be with me?'

'I needed it, Anya. I needed a new start.'

'So what is your new name?'

Again he didn't answer her and Anya knew he would not be allowed to reveal his new identity. He should not even be here as visiting the past was strictly forbidden.

'Roman.' Anya answered her own question, for he would always be Roman to her. Yes, maybe the details had changed but he was still Roman to her heart. The feelings she'd had for him had never left, now though they heightened.

'Are you still in the legion?'

'No.'

'How long were you there?'

'Ten years.'

Which would have brought him to twenty-eight, and, given he was almost thirty-two, it meant that there were four years missing.

'So, why are you here now?'

Because, despite so many promises to himself, he'd been unable to stay away.

'I had to see for myself that you are okay.'

'Then you'll leave?'

'Yes.'

He had to.

He did not want to complicate her life.

Always he had.

And he had read that she was dating Mika. He had always assumed male dancers were just pretty boys in tights.

His opinion had changed tonight.

'Anya, I just came to see that you were doing well and it is clear that you are.'

'Then go.'

Yet he did not.

They stood there, staring at each other, having a conversation, not with their mouths but with their eyes, just as they had in the early days. Then she would look across the sparse dining room and meet his solemn gaze.

Did you miss me? she asked without words.

His eyes told her that he had. They were black, the colour of coal, and they glinted the same way and could make her burn too.

His gaze moved down to her painted mouth and he would kiss her, she knew, because he had taken a tissue from her dressing table and was now removing her lipstick.

And she let him.

Even as he wiped off the crimson to expose the flesh of her lips, Roman knew he should walk away.

What the hell had he been thinking, that he could come and watch her dance and then simply leave?

Not a chance.

They were staring deep into each other's eyes and

their breathing was in the rhythm of the first time just before they had kissed.

Then Anya had come out of the stage door and faced Roman, then a man.

Tonight, though, as she put her hands up to his face, unlike then, he didn't flinch.

He just felt the soft probe of her fingers explore his face.

Such a beautiful face, Anya thought. High cheekbones, black eyes that were embedded in her mind and the lips that had taken her to heaven would let her glimpse it again now.

'I kiss you goodbye,' Roman said.

He did not say, *Can I kiss you?* Roman had never needed to ask.

His kiss was gentle and it surprised her for his kisses had previously been hot and rather rough. Now, though, he lowered his head and cupped her chin and softly kissed her lips, and they rediscovered each other. Anya's lips parted and he slipped his tongue into her mouth. They tasted each other, when they had starved for each other, but then he kissed her roughly again.

He pulled her tight into his body and she had never been held as Roman could hold her. He just owned her body and as her tutu was crushed against his suit his mouth ravaged hers.

He took her mouth in a deep, passionate kiss that made her hands move to his chest just to feel the strength and the power, never to push him away.

He pulled her harder into him. His hand was in the small of her back, warm and sensual, yet the barrier of the fabric of her tutu briefly halted it from moving lower.

It did not perturb him for long, and now his hand roamed her bottom.

Their tongues were mingling, their passion building, and it was a kiss that could no longer be classed as a farewell kiss for their bodies were greeting each other's again.

She could feel him pressed hard on her stomach, and his other hand now touched her breast, and though they rued the fabric that separated their skin, still it felt blissful. His thumb caressed her nipple and she ached for her breast to be naked in his hand.

'Tatania...' There was a knock at the door and she could hear the dresser wanting to come in.

They stopped kissing but still he held her, still he stroked her breast, and they stared into each other's eyes. She could feel his erection and, more than that, she could feel his body was broader, more primed, and she ached, simply ached for him, for the years he had denied her his touch, his body.

She should tell him to go, and now was her chance to do just that.

Roman knew too that he should leave.

Once, their eyes said.

Just this once.

Their bodies could kiss the other goodbye.

'I will deal with my costume,' Anya shouted through the door in Russian. 'You are to leave me.'

Roman would deal with her costume, Anya knew, as without a word he went and turned the key in the door.

He was back.

For *their* closing night.

# CHAPTER THREE

ANYA SHIVERED WITH want now, rather than stage fright.

Her legs, which had just a short while ago performed the most amazing feats, barely remembered how to walk as he took her by the hand and led her to the dressing-room chair. He moved it so that she faced to the side and he came round and got down on one knee.

He undid the silk ribbons of her pointe shoes and slipped them off, and Anya grimaced as he did so. Always, after a performance, it hurt to remove them.

There was blood on the toes of her ballet tights, even though she had worn in her shoes and bandaged her feet carefully. He caressed the soles of her feet and her sore heels and then he ran warm hands up her aching calves too.

Roman felt the cramped muscles beneath his fingers and he smoothed and soothed them for a couple of moments and Anya held onto his shoulder as she wished his hand would move higher.

'Come on,' he said in that deep low voice that made her throb, and as he stood so too did Anya and she lifted her arms.

Roman knew to be careful and his fingers found the small concealed zip and slid it down.

She stepped out of it and stood as he hung up her costume.

'Don't tell me I'm too thin…'

'Shh,' he said. He did not want to relive that final row. Instead he went to the waist of her ballet tights and slid them down. She was naked save for the bandages on her feet.

Again she sat on her dressing chair and he dealt with the bandages. Anya couldn't help herself, she reached and touched his gleaming black hair, unable to believe he was really here after all those years apart.

Still kneeling, he looked up and observed her body. He saw the small breasts and she closed her eyes as he licked at one and then blew, and then toyed with her nipple between his lips.

She held onto his head as he took her breast in his mouth and sucked and then did the same to the other, took it so deep that it hurt, and her thighs shook but his hands held them down.

'Roman…'

She was drunk on him, aching to be with him, and when he removed his mouth she caught her breath and watched as he parted her thighs and looked at her. Oh, she ached for him to bury his head there but he stroked her for a moment and slipped his fingers inside and then ran a figure of eight with one damp finger around her clitoris. They smiled at the memory of their first time and her telling him where it was.

Roman had cared only for his pleasure back then.

At first.

Then he had discovered the sanctuary of her bliss.

Now he removed his finger and stood.

She could see his erection and then she felt it for herself, running her hand over and over it as he unbuckled his belt. She took it out as he removed his tie and undid the buttons of his shirt so his chest was bare, but he left his shirt and jacket on.

Such beauty, she thought as she licked her lips and lowered her head to take just one small taste.

That turned into more.

The feathers of her headdresses moved and shivered and teased against his toned stomach, soft and tender, unlike the feel of her skilled mouth that gave rapid flicks and enslaved him. Roman's breathing tripped into a moan that was a familiar one and turned Anya on totally.

She took him deeper but now more slowly as his fingers worked the pins of her headdress and, care forgotten, he tossed it aside and pushed her head lower.

His fingers were busy freeing her hair, and then he lifted her head. He was so close to coming and she licked her lips. He raised her, lifted her body against his and kicked away the chair. He brushed away all her carefully placed trinkets in one motion and then placed her on the dressing table. Anya stroked him as he carefully angled the mirrors so that there were hundreds of them and then he pulled her bottom to the edge of the table and parted her legs, and in his deep gravelly voice he told her that he was going to fill her with ecstasy.

He did.

Anya gripped tight to the edge of the table and arched back as he drove in.

He tore into her and the pain and bliss of their first time was replicated.

Roman had always loved to watch them, and now he looked down and widened her legs for better exposure, so that he could see himself glide in and out.

Anya looked at the mirror.

There they were, an endless stretch of Anyas and Romans but there were hundreds of images when instead there should be hundreds of memories, all denied to her by him.

'I hate you for leaving,' she sobbed as he started to thrust faster into her, and then she pressed her lips together so she would not reveal more of her hurt.

He did not look to the mirrors, he simply looked down and then when he had to have her body closer, he scooped her in to him and her skin was against his naked chest as her mouth found his.

Anya wrapped her legs around him and she was no longer on the table. She moved on him, and for all she had danced tonight, she did so again. Gripping him, grinding herself on him, wrapping toned legs tightly to his loins, and she held on as his powerful thighs allowed him to thrust harder.

She was fit enough not to require holding and now Roman's large hands cupped her buttocks and he stroked them in deep rhythm till she shivered from the inside.

'Stay still…' he told her.

'I can't.'

'I want to feel you.'

He knew she was almost there and now his hands held her rigid and would not allow her to move. He knew her body, and he was right, because as he held her still she felt him swell and he let out a primal grunt as he did what he had promised, filled her with ecstasy. The feel of him coming long and deep into her brought Anya to her own intense climax. It raced the length of her spine, she seized in his arms and pulsed and dragged out from him every precious drop and ached as still she fought for more.

They kissed and even now, Anya knew, she could have him again.

Such was their endless desire that, as they rested their foreheads on each other, Anya knew she could bring him back with just a few shifts of her hips—they could resume and chase oblivion again.

Their mouths meshed and their tongues mingled as her hips did just that, and she gripped and massaged him back, but there was knocking at the door.

Anya closed her eyes in frustration as she was informed that the car would soon be there to take her to the after party.

Their lips parted in regret and as Roman lowered her she never wanted her feet to hit the floor, but they did. She rested her head on his chest and drank in the scent of him, of them.

'Did you love me?'

Anya had to know but he did not answer.

Almost fourteen years later and she still didn't know.

Fourteen years without seeing him.

Only that wasn't quite true, as he regularly appeared in her dreams.

But, no, there had been that one time she had seen him since then. It was something she had tried to erase from her memory.

A sight she would have preferred never to have seen.

Yet she had.

She looked up at his mouth, at his slight smile, and Anya knew how rare a smile from Roman was.

But then she looked into his eyes and was there a glint of triumph there?

Was that a smug smile at how easily he could have

her? That, after all these years, he could walk back in and she would melt like a candle to his flame?

And she was angry at him, and perhaps more angry at herself for just how readily she had succumbed. Anger took over then.

Anya knew what she had seen two years ago.

On seeing him again there had been little relief that the man she loved hadn't died on a battlefield.

There had been rage instead and it resurfaced now.

She raised her hand and slapped him, and he took it without so much as a flinch.

And then she asked him what perhaps she should have asked earlier.

'How's your wife?'

# CHAPTER FOUR

YES, SHE SHOULD have asked earlier.

But this was how their love had always been, so consuming and so intense that there wasn't room for anything else other than them.

Roman was sure that had Anya been married and a mother of triplets, had she been working on the checkout, still their first meeting, after all these years apart, it would have been the same.

They *had* to have each other.

It was why he had let her go.

'You know?' Roman frowned. 'How?'

'I saw you in Paris, two years ago, when I was performing there,' Anya said. 'You were sitting in a square, having a drink with her at a café and kissing in the afternoon sun...' It had been agony to see and it was agony now to recall it. She had been rushing from her hotel to the theatre to prepare for her performance. She had progressed to being a soloist and had been playing the part of Violente, one of the fairies in *Sleeping Beauty*, and had been an understudy for the Lilac Fairy, who'd played a major role in the dance.

That night, for the first time, she would be performing as the Lilac Fairy, and it had been the only thing on her mind until Anya had turned into the square and her brisk pace had come to a rapid halt.

It was Roman.

Absolutely it was.

She had stood, frozen.

Roman had been sitting at a pavement café in the late-afternoon sun, and though her heart had recognised him she had not understood the exquisitely dressed man who'd lounged in the chair. Or why there had been a middle-aged woman by his side.

Her throat had closed and her jaw had gritted as she'd watched the woman reach over and kiss him.

The glint of her wedding ring had caused Anya to frown and, for a brief moment, she had assumed that Roman was having an affair with an older, married woman.

That had caused enough pain in itself but then, with the kiss over, she had watched as he'd lifted his cup and everything in her world had seemed to dim as she'd seen that there was a ring on *his* finger.

The cry she had let out had gone unnoticed by passers-by. Actually, no, as she now properly recalled it, a woman had turned her head as she'd walked past.

And then, when she'd thought her heart had died, Anya had found out that it was, in fact, being tortured as Roman, *her* brooding, distant, lover, had taken his wife's hand and held it and they'd shared a kiss again.

She had wanted to scream in rage, to dash over and stop them. To demand of Roman how the hell he could cheat on her. For that was exactly how it had felt—as if she had caught him having an affair.

Yet she'd been unable to bring herself to confront him. She'd been tempted to run back to the tiny hotel room, to lie on her bed and sob, such was her grief, but that night's performance was a vital one.

For the first time in her life Anya had truly thought she could not perform. On the most vital night of her career to date, she had doubted that she could go on.

Somehow she had made it to the theatre and taken out all her tiny keepsakes, her earring, the foil from the chocolate and the label from the sheet.

Oh, she had thought about tossing them; instead she had wept on them, grieved *again* for the two of them.

But then she had risen.

Anya, that night, had danced better than she ever had, though her fury, to this day, remained.

'So,' Anya demanded as she wrapped a robe around herself and Roman did up his clothes, 'how is she? Does she wait backstage…' She looked at his immaculate suit. 'She dresses her plaything well…'

'My money is mine,' Roman said.

'Please…' she scoffed. 'You had nothing.'

'When I knew you,' Roman said, 'I had nothing. I made my fortune myself.'

'Rubbish—you found a rich wife. I saw her sitting there, dripping in jewels. So, tell me, how is she?'

'She *was* wonderful,' Roman said, and let her know in those words that his wife had died and that he would defend not just his late wife but the indefensible fact that he'd had another woman after Anya. 'Don't speak poorly of her again, Anya, or you shan't like my response.'

A violent drenching of jealousy flooded Anya as he spoke.

'Celeste died a year ago.'

There were two things that Anya hated about that statement.

That she knew his wife's name and that she had died a year ago yet *still* he hadn't sought her out.

But, then, what did she expect? Neither had he sought out his identical twin. Roman was the coldest, most complex of men, his dark eyes had always held mystery and she stared into them now.

'Did you know I was performing in Paris, then?'

'I did.'

'Did you come and see me?' Anya asked, for always she danced for him.

'No,' Roman said. 'Celeste wanted to but I made an excuse not to go and she went with a friend.'

'Why?'

He didn't want to answer.

Roman knew exactly the night Anya referred to. He and Celeste had been sitting at a pavement café and waiting for her friend to arrive.

'Why don't you want to come to the ballet?' Celeste had asked.

'I just…' He had shrugged.

'We're breaking up, aren't we?' Celeste had reached over and kissed him. 'It's okay, Roman, we agreed to two years.'

And those two years would have soon been over. But Celeste had just found out that she was seriously ill and had had only six months to live.

He had taken a drink of his coffee and his decision had been made.

'I'm not leaving you to face this alone.'

He had taken her hand.

'I'll be with you all the way through this,' he had promised, and it had been sealed with a tender kiss.

A kiss that, it turned out, Anya had witnessed.

'Why?' Anya demanded. 'Why did you not come and see me perform? Didn't you care?'

'No,' Roman said. 'I promised that I would be faithful to my wife. To watch you dance would have felt like an affair.'

It was the only glimpse he gave her that, through the years, feelings had remained.

She didn't understand him and he gave her nothing that might bring her closer to doing so. 'Why haven't you told Daniil that you are in London?' Anya challenged.

'You don't know that I haven't.'

'Yes, I do because I was at Daniil's this afternoon,' Anya said.

Roman said nothing but she saw his jaw grit as she made it clear that she and his brother were in touch.

'He is married…' she told him.

'I read in the news.'

'They have a new baby.'

'I read about that too.'

'He still searches for you,' Anya said. 'He doesn't know if you are alive or dead.'

'Did you not tell him that you saw me in Paris?'

'No,' Anya said. She hadn't told Daniil because she wished that she had never seen Roman sitting in the sun and kissing a woman that had not been her. 'Perhaps I shall tell him next time I see him,' she taunted. 'Did you know that your niece gets christened next Sunday?'

She watched as his eyes shuttered.

'You might have erased your past when you joined the legion but we all live on. Your niece's name is Nadia…'

'Anya…' He put up his hand to halt her but she refused to be silenced.

'Oh, and Sev will be there, with his new wife Naomi…'

She could hear his heavy breathing as she bombarded him with names from his past.

People he had loved yet had chosen to never contact again.

'Nikolai is coming. You remember he loved ships, well, he has a superyacht now...'

'You lie,' Roman said. 'Don't you remember?' He looked at her. 'Of course not, you were off at dance school, but Nikolai ran away and committed suicide.'

They had been such dark, painful times. Roman could still remember the night that they had been informed that Nikolai's body had been pulled from the river.

He had asked if he might speak with Sev, because he'd known that he would be devastated. After all, Nikolai and Sev had been best friends.

That request had been denied and Roman had been locked in his room instead. He hadn't cried, he hadn't even known how to, but that night, thinking of the torture that must have been in Nikolai's head, he had been the closest he had ever come to breaking down.

Now Anya was here, telling him that Nikolai was alive.

'Nikolai ran away, but the body they pulled from the river wasn't his,' Anya said.

Roman kept his feelings hidden—he always had—and his time in the legion had honed that skill, but hearing Nikolai was alive, that all his friends would be together next Sunday, meant it took everything he possessed to keep his voice level.

'And shall you be there?'

Anya nodded. 'I am coming back from Paris just for the day.'

'Coming back?'

'We go there tomorrow.'

'We?'

'The dance company.'

He wanted to ask about Mika, yet he did not.

Tonight was a one-night stand, for old times' sake, Roman told himself.

There was another knock on the door, and they were told that the car was there to take her to her leaving party.

'It can wait!' Anya called back.

'You ought to go,' he said. 'Or you'll have your mother calling me a saboteur again.'

'She died, Roman,' Anya said. 'And please don't offer a false apology.'

'I shan't.'

He hated Katya, more than even Anya could know.

'I will leave you to get ready for your party.'

'So we just have sex and you leave?' she challenged, and then she gave a derisive laugh. 'Nothing changes, does it?'

She watched as he checked his reflection in the mirror. She knew it was for her sake, walking out wearing her make-up would not be a good look, but his unruffled demeanour incensed her.

He smoothed his hair back and straightened his tie, and with a tissue he removed a little of her make-up that had smeared onto his face.

As he went to give her cheek a kiss Anya pulled her head back, but just as he reached the door she called him back.

There was something she just had to know.

'How did you meet your wife?'

'It doesn't matter,' Roman said.

'It does to me. I want to know,' she said. 'Was it love

at first sight, or was it her money you wanted? Tell me, Roman, how did you meet?'

'I answered an advert. She was looking for a husband.'

And with that sordid revelation he might as well have ripped out her heart and stamped on it. Rather than search for her, he had simply answered an ad.

'Bastard!'

'Yep,' Roman said.

'You're a whore, Roman,' Anya swore. 'I hate you.'

'Why?' he asked. 'Because I made a life for myself?'

She did not answer. Yes, she hated him for making a life that did not include her and she would never forgive him for marrying another woman. 'Come on, Anya.' He touched on a subject he did not necessarily want to discuss. 'Don't tell me you haven't seen anyone.'

'Of course I have,' she said. 'Do you really think I kept myself on ice for you?'

She lied.

There had been no one else.

Dance was all she had.

She had not just kept herself on ice, she had turned into it. No one could ever come close to the memory of him and so she held onto it and held back from others.

'It was good to see you, Roman,' she said. 'Please don't expect a repeat performance in Paris. I would prefer it if you stayed away.' She turned to head to the shower, but then changed her mind. 'You need to let your twin know you are alive, or I shall. You chose to reappear,' she said. 'I shan't keep any secrets for you from now on.' She told him Daniil's address. 'He changed his name a couple of years ago, so that you might find him. I can't believe you have not spent every day searching for him.'

Then she looked at a man who had simply turned his

back on the life they could have had, and, yes, actually she could believe it.

'I hope she was worth it.'

'Worth what?'

The end of them.

'Go,' Anya said.

She wanted him to leave now.

And, because it was Roman, just like that, he went.

It was pride that stopped her calling him back.

She stepped into the shower and quickly dressed for her after party.

Blasting her hair with the dryer, it fell softly around her face. Her hands were still shaking from their brief reunion.

She pulled on a pale grey dress and some heels and then headed out.

Colour she saved for the stage.

'Where were you?' Mika asked, as she climbed into the limousine to head to the hotel where the party was being held.

'I had people to greet.'

They sat in silence, Anya lost in her thoughts. Mika was sulking at being kept waiting and he read what was being said on social media about tonight's performance. They ignored each other but as they stepped out onto the red carpet they came alive again, for it added to the mystery of the dance world. There were screams for Mika, because he had quite a fangirl following. Mika, though, put a protective arm around Anya and they smiled for the cameras and then headed inside.

Instead of refusing the delicacies that were being offered, as she usually did, Anya took a serviette and a small beignet and bit into the warm, sweet dough.

There were a few raised eyebrows when she took another and then another. The lemon in her water was her usual fuel for this type of thing.

But sex had made her hungry, or was it that Roman was back?

Yes, the people around could see the changes. Not just that she ate but that her cheeks were pink and her green eyes glittered.

After all these years, her body felt alive again and yet he had killed her soul.

The next morning as the famed ballet troupe headed for a snatched week at home or straight on to Paris before rehearsals began in earnest, Anya fought with herself not to stop the car and get out.

Roman was in London.

And as she sat on the plane and strapped on her seat belt she wanted to disembark. It felt wrong to be leaving when he was here.

She turned away from the chatter of colleagues and stared out of the window and thought of Roman and Daniil catching up after all these years, and then she thought of what had taken place last night.

Then, despite harsh words to Roman and a brutal lecture to herself, insisting that she was through with him, she consoled herself with one thought.

She would see him at the christening, she was sure.

It wasn't over.

It never had been.

# CHAPTER FIVE

ROMAN AWOKE ON the morning of the christening and as he lay there he was hit with an unfamiliar feeling—he wanted to be waking up in his Parisian home.

Roman was not used to missing a city, or a building, but as he got up and showered he was glad that soon he would be going home.

Today, though, he would meet with Daniil.

He still hadn't contacted him.

The natural assumption might be that he would want to see his identical twin before seeing Anya.

The assumption would have been wrong.

He and Daniil had been abandoned at approximately two weeks of age. No one knew who had been born first but it had always been assumed that Roman was the elder.

Roman had been a natural leader and, though Daniil was as tough as they came, Roman had looked out for his brother at every turn. He had taken care of him and taken the fall for him and had wanted only the best for his twin.

When Daniil had been adopted Roman had made a promise to himself that he was letting his twin go for good.

Daniil had had a chance, a real chance for a good life

and an entirely new start, and Roman had insisted that he take it.

When Daniil had refused to leave, when he had reminded Roman that they would make it themselves as boxers, Roman had told him he would do better without him, that he was the better fighter and that it was Daniil, if he stayed, who would drag him down.

A forbidden fight had been set up in the dorm and Roman had fought dirty that night.

'See, *shishka*,' Roman had said. Daniil had been recovering from a savage blow that had ripped apart his cheek and Roman had used the name they had called him since they had found out he was to be adopted. It meant big shot. 'I do better without you.'

So Daniil had taken his chance. There had been no letters sent from England to the orphanage, no attempt by Daniil to contact his twin. Though Roman had missed him, the knowledge that his brother had a chance had consoled him.

When Roman had left the orphanage he had considered trying to track Daniil down, but the thought of turning up on his doorstep, of being a burden on his twin, meant he had decided to leave well alone.

Roman had considered it again when he had come out of the French Foreign Legion. Unlike most legionnaires, he had amassed quite a fortune thanks to a long conversation with a comrade, Dario.

The men had rarely spoken about their lives before joining the legion—it was what they had come to get away from after all. But one night in the desert, both wounded and waiting for help to arrive, they had touched on their pasts.

'Stay awake,' Roman said as Dario slipped in and out

of consciousness. Roman too wanted the bliss of closing his eyes but he knew it would have signalled the end. The sand in his lacerated back felt as if salt was being rubbed into his wounds, and he could hear the gurgle of his chest as he tried to breathe. He held onto the gold earring he had taken from his pocket and it felt as if Anya was by his side and for her he kept his eyes open. 'Dario!' he commanded. 'Talk.'

Silence.

'What are you thinking about?' Roman asked.

'My wife,' Dario said. 'I left chaos behind me,' he admitted to Roman. 'I just hope she is okay.'

They conversed in French, as was the rule.

'If I'd stayed I'd have been locked up, I think,' Dario said. 'What about you?'

'I don't know.' Roman tried to imagine what life might have been like had he stayed. He might have moved to Saint Petersburg but he could not imagine things going well there. How would he have supported Anya? He couldn't have.

He thought of the furious words that Katya had hurled at him. Anya's audition hadn't gone well and the blame, her mother had said, lay squarely with him.

'I tried it as a boxer but got nowhere,' Roman told his wounded comrade.

'You're a good boxer,' Dario commented, because Roman was in the parachute regiment kickboxing team.

'I knew nothing about nutrition then,' Roman said. 'Anyway, getting beaten up for a living never really appealed. It was just a dream when we were growing up—a way out.'

'We?'

Roman didn't answer that question.

'I was good at the share market,' Dario said. 'I got rich but then I got foolish.'

'Foolish?'

'I didn't stick to the rules,' he admitted. 'You have to know when to hold steady, know when to pull out.'

And Dario told Roman the rules that he had failed to adhere to and he told him about brokers and such things. Recovering in Provence, Roman had set things in motion.

Legionnaires' board and lodging were provided and Roman had barely touched his wage so he set it to work. He was attached to nothing and no one, certainly not money, and he had way more self-discipline than most. These were the perfect ingredients to play the stock market and Roman did it incredibly well.

Having recovered from his injuries, Roman signed on for another five years but he would leave the legion a wealthy man. Still, there were things he did not know about and had never experienced and he was embarrassed to go to his brother. The night before he walked out of the gates he and his comrades had drunk plenty. They would miss Roman and could not imagine a better solider beside them in battle, or a more focused, determined person to get them there on long, seemingly endless marches. He had done all he could to never leave a comrade behind.

'What about this one…?' Dario said. They were reading the personal ads. 'If I was leaving this is where I'd be headed. I don't know about going to the ballet and theatre, but the adventurous sex I could do with…'

Roman smiled as he read it.

She was in her early forties and lived in Paris. No name was provided, just that she had given up on finding love but wanted to marry to please her dying father.

She wanted someone, preferably younger and attractive, to accompany her on nights out to the theatre and ballet. As well as that she wanted an adventurous sexual partner. She understood that the marriage might not be a long one but hoped it would last at least two years. Naturally accommodation would be provided and she was an excellent cook, though preferred to eat out in the evening.

He liked her directness.

Throughout his life Roman had always had board and lodgings provided, first as an orphan, then as a fighter and perhaps now as a lover!

The men had whooped in delight when he had pocketed the details and even Roman had grinned.

Responding to the advert was a calculated move. He had never lived in a home, let alone been to the theatre. On a rare day off he might have hit a bar with comrades but he had never been to a restaurant except for that one disastrous time with Anya.

Roman headed to Paris.

Yes, he had been right not to contact his twin, Roman soon found out as he tried to acclimatise to living in an apartment in Paris and sharing a bed. Even lingering over meals proved difficult—he been nowhere near ready to face Daniil.

After those awkward first weeks things improved. More than delighted with happenings in the bedroom, Celeste wanted to venture out. She loved the job of 'improving' Roman. She had an eye for fashion and he was dressed well. He learnt to eat from fine china and to order at a restaurant with ease. She cooked with passion and soon so too did he. He always spent his own money, yet Celeste knew real estate in Paris and soon his portfolio consisted of houses as well as shares, though, as was the case with his shares, he was not attached to any of the properties.

And the sex?

There was a lot of it, of course, but, although it started out risqué, tenderness and affection grew, so much so that when, at the end of two years, Celeste fell ill, Roman stayed in the marriage. Just as he'd done all he could to never leave a comrade behind, he remained by her side. He was now the teacher, showing her that with focus and determination six months to live could be turned into a year.

'You are the best thing that ever happened to me,' Celeste said just before she died.

Her estate naturally went to her sister, who had blinked in surprise that Roman had not contested the will.

Of course they had assumed he had been there for the money.

Not for a moment.

He had been there for the education: to somehow transition from a life lived in regimented institutions or war zones to the real world.

After her death he left the hotel he had checked into and went to look at a property in the Eighth District in Paris to add to his portfolio. Taking the antique elevator to the top floor, he walked into the magnificent apartment and felt something he had never felt before. The very French furnishings, the stunning view of Paris, the wraparound balcony all appealed. So much so that for the first time he felt attached to a building and had bought it to live in. But more than that he finally felt a part of the planet he lived on and he was ready to consider contacting his brother.

Almost.

Daniil had been adopted by a rich English family. Roman had read that he had married an English woman and so, as he was only able to converse in Russian and French, Roman had spent the last few months learning English.

He was ready to face his twin now.

The brother he had sworn to let go forever.

He would not be a burden.

Roman took out a suit and dressed and he did up his tie with steady hands.

They only shook slightly as he opened the hotel safe.

He had found a Russian jeweller.

There he had seen a stone in the palest of greens and it had reminded him of Anya's eyes.

Yet the gift he'd had made for his niece was a platinum cross studded with diamonds and on the back the word *Sila* had been engraved in Cyrillic. It was the Russian word for strength. This was not a trinket to be worn— more, if need arose, and his niece ever fell on hard times, it was insurance.

Money was all he had to give.

He didn't even know if he was ready to get in touch with Daniil but he had taken seriously Anya's warning that she would no longer pretend she hadn't seen him. So, on the morning of the christening, he was driven to the address Anya had given and entered an impressive foyer.

The doorman nodded.

'Good morning, Mr Zverev.'

It had been a long time since that had happened, Roman thought.

In the orphanage they had always been mixed up and had often used it to their advantage.

'I didn't do it,' they would say separately. 'You're mistaking me for him.'

'Well, your brother says that it must have been you.'

This morning Roman used it to his advantage again and headed for the elevator and pressed the button that would take him to Daniil's penthouse suite.

Roman had fought in the harshest of conditions and had witnessed the hell of the front line but now he was nervous.

As he had stood watching Anya curtsey to the duchess and knowing he would soon see her, Roman had felt his heart pounding in his chest, and it was pounding in the same way now. He knocked on a large wooden door and after a few moments it opened. A blonde woman stood there and her expression showed that not only did she recognise him, she was shocked.

'Daniil!'

She called her husband, her tone urgent, and then she blinked rapidly as if she had suddenly remembered she had forgotten to greet him. 'Roman, we've been looking for you,' she said, and stepped towards Roman and embraced him.

A few years ago he would have recoiled but Celeste had taught him well and so he accepted the embrace.

'I'm Libby,' the woman said, and stepped back.

Roman could see that there were tears in her eyes.

'I know this is a shock,' Roman said in English. His English accent was a mixture of French and Russian. 'Congratulations on the birth of your daughter. I have a gift…' And then his voice trailed off as she turned to her husband, who was coming down the hall.

They were absolutely identical. It was almost like

looking into a mirror except Daniil had the livid scar on his cheek that Roman had put there.

'Where the hell have you been?' Daniil said by way of greeting. 'I thought you were dead…'

'Well, I'm not,' Roman said.

There could be no warm, effusive greeting after all these years; there was too much pain and far too many questions before they could even begin to hope for that.

'I hear that you have had a baby. Congratulations.'

'Her name is Nadia,' Daniil said.

Even within that brief exchange Roman could hear his own heavy accent compared to his twin's, and simply for ease he continued in their native tongue and asked his brother how he was. *'Kak dela?'*

'We shall speak in English in front of my wife,' Daniil snapped.

'Daniil?' Libby frowned, clearly a bit stunned at her husband's reaction, but Daniil did not stop to explain the unexpected wash of agony that tempered his relief that his brother was alive; instead he asked Roman the vital question again.

'Where the hell have you been?'

Roman didn't answer.

'Where do you live?' Daniil pushed.

'Paris.'

'And how long have you lived there?'

'Several years.'

'That's an hour away!' Daniil said, and he fronted his brother as if ready to fight him. 'You live an hour away and yet you haven't been in touch.'

'Daniil.' Libby raised her voice and then tried to speak in a more normal tone. 'Come in, Roman.'

It was a beautiful apartment and a gorgeous view of

London played out before them through glass walls—the city sparkled in the early morning sun yet the atmosphere in the room was as tense as Roman had expected it to be.

He took a seat and it was odd seeing Daniil grown up when he was still twelve years old in Roman's head. They were incredibly similar except for the scar and Roman was surprised that Daniil hadn't had cosmetic surgery on it.

'You need to get that taken care of,' he said, pointing to his own cheek .

'I kept it to remind me of you.' Daniil's response was bitter. 'It's all I had.'

'No,' Roman refuted. 'Didn't you get the pictures that I put in your case?'

Daniil nodded. Roman remembered slipping them into his twin's case just before he'd headed to England.

'I've been searching for you,' Daniil said. 'I've been back to Russia several times and someone said that you had been talking of joining the foreign legion.'

'I joined when I was eighteen. I served for ten years.'

'And so what is your name now?' Daniil asked, but Roman wouldn't answer him. 'Pierre?' Daniil's sneer as he guessed at a French name told Roman how angry he was that his brother had changed his identity. 'You're not going to tell me, are you?'

Roman wasn't, only not for the reason Daniil assumed.

In the foreign legion everyone, on joining, was given a new identity but what Daniil and Anya clearly didn't know was that at the end of the first year legionnaires could choose whether to continue with their new identity or revert back to their own.

When Roman had joined, it had been his intention to wipe his slate clean. But a year on, on the eve of making the decision, he had lain on his bed, his hands behind his head, staring at the ceiling and deep in thought.

And had decided he couldn't do it.

He had survived the most brutal training, he had jumped from planes, had become fluent in French, he'd had comrades and purpose. Everything that he had hoped to attain from joining he had.

His contract then had been for five years and he would sign up again, and yet when the moment had come, he couldn't bring himself to make that final turn of the key and close himself from the past.

If he'd maintained his new identity the rules would have had to be adhered to and he'd been a soldier trained to obey. It would have meant never making any sort of contact with Daniil.

Or Anya.

The night they had shared last week could never have taken place.

This morning could never have happened.

Yet if he told Daniil or Anya this, it would show them how much he needed them, but he did not want to invade their lives so he said nothing.

'That fight.' Daniil had a question. 'It was to make me go, wasn't it?'

'You wouldn't have left otherwise.'

'I didn't want to go.'

'Look at all you have. The family you went to—' Roman started, but Daniil suddenly stood.

'I was sent to hell!' he told Roman. 'I was a replacement for their dead child.'

Roman just sat there unmoved. 'You got a good education.'

'*Poshyol ty...*' Daniil swore at his brother in Russian.

'I thought we were supposed to speak English in front of your wife,' Roman calmly reminded him.

'You don't know what it was like...' Daniil said.

'Because you never wrote and told me.'

Oh, there was so much hurt on both sides.

'I did, but I've since found out that my adopted parents never sent the letters. I changed my name from Daniel Thomas back to Daniil Zverev just so that you could find me.'

'I saw that you did.'

'When?'

'Last year.'

'And still you waited?'

Oh, no! Libby thought as she sat there, bemused by their reactions. She knew how hard Daniil had searched for his twin and simply didn't understand. She wanted hugs and champagne and smiling Russians.

This wasn't how it was supposed to be!

'I'll get the baby!' she said, and dashed out and returned with a tiny sleeping infant in her arms, hoping that Nadia would work her magic.

'How old is she?' Roman asked as Libby came back.

'Two weeks,' Libby said.

That was the age he and Daniil had been when they had been left at the orphanage.

Or the guessed age.

'You can hold her,' Libby said.

'No.' Roman shook his head. 'Let her sleep.'

But Libby put the baby in his arms.

He had never held one.

'She's very light,' Roman said, and then the baby stirred and opened her eyes and she recognised the eyes that stared back at her as her father's.

She was absolutely beautiful and she looked a combination of both Libby and Daniil, and of course that meant she looked as if she could almost be his. It was odd, he had never imagined himself a father, or Daniil come to that. Now, he looked at the tiny infant and felt a rush of emotion and also relief to see her so safe and cared for and to know his brother had done well and would take very good care of his wife and child.

Roman was doing everything he could to get through these days. Catching up with his past was agony, and to hold her for even a moment longer meant he might break down.

He had never shed a tear.

Not one.

And he would not now.

He handed Nadia back to Libby and then he stood and got to the reason he was there.

'I had this made for Nadia.' He went to hand over the box to Libby but Daniil intervened.

'She gets christened in an hour. You can give it to her after the service. We are all coming back here for a small celebration.'

'I can't attend the christening.'

'I don't give a damn about your new identity and whether you can be seen out or not with us,' Daniil said. 'You will be at your niece's christening.'

Roman said nothing.

'Nikolai will be there and so too will Sev—he married a couple of weeks ago but he's returning from his honeymoon just to attend. He's made the effort to be there and so too will you. We are all getting together on Nikolai's yacht afterwards. The four of us will be together again.'

They had once all been so close.

'Anya might be coming to the christening. You remember her...' Daniil said. 'The cook's daughter who always danced?'

'Vaguely.'

'She's a prima ballerina now.' Daniil said what Roman already knew.

'And she was almost Nadia's godmother,' Libby sighed, and Roman frowned.

'You're that close?'

'Not really,' Libby admitted. 'Well, we're all ballet dancers...'

'All?'

'My friend Rachel and I, but Anya keeps herself apart.'

'Is that how you met her?' Roman asked. He was curious while trying not to let on that he knew Anya intimately. 'You have danced together?'

'No, no,' Libby said. 'I retired last year and Daniil took me to the ballet to cheer me up.'

'It didn't work,' Daniil said in a dry voice.

'Well,' Libby continued, 'Daniil recognised Anya from the program and we went backstage and we've kept in touch since then. We weren't sure if Rachel could be there today and Anya had offered to step in as godmother. I found out last night that Rachel can make it after all. I think I've offended Anya, so she might not come.'

The intercom buzzed. It would seem that the caterers had arrived and Libby gave a yelp when she saw the time.

'I have to get Nadia changed. Roman...' Libby took a breath. 'You are coming to the christening?'

Roman hesitated. The fact Anya might not be there made it easier so he nodded.

Alone with his twin, for a moment before the caterers invaded and the christening day took hold, they stared at the other then Roman spoke. 'I'll let you get ready and see you at the church.'

'Come in the car with us.'

'I've got my own driver.'

'Don't disappear again, Roman,' Daniil warned.

He couldn't if he tried.

Now that contact had been made, he wanted to be in their lives.

'You're a curse, Roman.' He thought of Katya's words. 'A burden on the system. You're not even suitable for adoption, what family would want you in it?'

His?

Roman had to be sure.

# CHAPTER SIX

As Anya climbed out of the taxi her eyes scanned the gathered crowd outside the church but there was no sign of him.

He wasn't here.

She had flown in from Paris that morning and had booked a return flight for this afternoon to safeguard her from a night in bed with Roman.

As if that would stop them!

Everyone had made the effort—Sev and Naomi, who lived in New York, had returned from their honeymoon for today. Nikolai, who had come to London only for their wedding, had delayed his departure to celebrate today. Even Rachel, who until last night hadn't known if she'd be able to get out of a family arrangement, had made it.

Yet Roman hadn't.

Anya was angry.

Furious.

As she walked towards the group she made a beeline for Rachel. She was a stunning redhead who had recently retired as a dancer and had just started a blog about ballet. Anya had been alerted to it when she had checked her emails and had read it on the plane. To cover her disappointment, she smiled rather more brightly than she would usually.

'I read your piece,' Anya said. 'It was amazing. Rachel, I will be in touch and we'll have to see what we can do about tickets for opening night...'

Rachel had been fishing for them at Sev and Naomi's wedding and Anya had blanked her.

She was trying not to be like that now.

Always she kept herself contained. Anya didn't make friends easily, but she was starting to care deeply about these people who had come into her life since the night Daniil and Libby had come backstage.

She was terrified of opening up and letting anyone in, just to be hurt in the end.

Now, since Roman had returned it had become increasingly hard to keep herself in check and to cast feelings and emotions aside.

She could see Rachel's surprise at the turnaround in her. Anya was surprised too but that was what Roman did, he changed her.

One night with him and she was turning back into her more emotional self.

They made their way over to the group.

'Hi, Anya.' Libby smiled, but Anya could see she that was tense.

And then she found out why as a car pulled up and Roman climbed out.

'He turned up this morning,' Libby said, though more to Rachel, her close friend, than to Anya. 'It didn't exactly go well.'

'Oh...' Rachel said. 'Isn't he the missing one?'

Libby gave a brief shake of her head, as if to say, It's too complicated for now.

In contrast, Anya thought now was a *very* good time and made good on her promise that she would no longer cover for Roman and pretend she didn't know where he had been all these years. Her voice was one of pure malice. 'He was never missing. He's been in Paris.'

'You knew where he was?' Libby accused. 'And you didn't tell Daniil…'

But Anya just shrugged. 'You've heard of Russian mail-order brides?' She sneered. 'Roman was a mail-order groom to some bored, rich, middle-aged woman in Paris…'

'He's married?' Daniil's voice was like the crack of a whip and he didn't wait for Anya's response. Instead along with Nikolai and Sev they walked towards Roman and for the first time in years they were together again.

Anya watched as they greeted each other with handshakes—the four beautiful men that she had grown up alongside were finally reunited.

For as long as she could remember, one of them had had her heart.

Anya was holding onto it with all she had today.

She always dressed neutrally, but never more so than this morning. Her dress was sand-coloured, her shoes flat and she wore a thin cardigan to cover her arms. What was considered beautiful on stage at times drew whispers and stares so she covered up when out.

Anya would not let Roman think for a moment she had made an extra effort for him.

Her week in Paris so far had been hell.

There had been no formal practice as some of the dancers had gone home to Russia before preparations began seriously.

Anya had tortured herself first by going to the square

where she had seen Roman with Celeste. She had then gone to the café, sat at the same table and ordered a meal, telling herself she would get back on the diet wagon tomorrow.

Instead she had wandered the streets, imagining him here.

With his wife.

It would hurt forever

And she had sat at another café and eaten crepes, trying to fathom that Roman lived here.

And now back in London she stood silently watching the four men converse. She was torn between longing and anger as she looked at him and he pointedly didn't meet her gaze.

In fact, he then turned his back to her.

'Let's go in,' Libby said, and finally they moved into the church. Anya found herself sitting with Rachel and in the pew behind Roman.

He had offered not a single word of greeting.

Carry on ignoring me, Anya thought as her eyes almost stripped the skin from his neck, and after a moment he turned and his eyes and the set of his lips told her how cross he was.

'Thanks so much for your discretion back there.' He spoke to her in terse Russian. 'I hadn't yet told Daniil I was married.'

Anya just gave a scoffing laugh. 'Rachel asked where you'd been, so I told her. Why would I lie for you, Roman?'

'I'll deal with you later.'

'You wish.' Anya smirked.

And then she saw it, the slight roll of his tongue in his cheek as he resisted a smile.

For that was them.

They knew their dance.

Except, Anya vowed, this time it would not end in bed.

Been there, done that, Anya's eyes warned him, and I am so not going there again.

Yes, if people thought her cold, this man was the reason.

She had loved him.

With all her heart she had loved him and had thought foolishly that he had loved her back.

The service was beautiful.

But hell for both of them.

Anya could hardly stand to look at the baby.

Nadia.

Thanks to a life spent on a diet, and it had been even more strict these past two years, a baby was something she could never have. Over and over she told herself she didn't want to be a mother, anyway. But watching Daniil, at the end of the service, hold his daughter brought a lump to her throat for the other thing, apart from Roman, that she could not have.

Yes, it was hard for both of them.

Watching his twin, clearly in love, perhaps made a mockery of what he and Celeste had had and Daniil had indicated he was furious that Roman had not told him about his wife.

Roman, who had never explained himself to anyone, did not know how to discuss it.

They spilled out of the church and into various cars and Anya quickly accepted an offer to ride with Naomi and Sev. She had only seen Naomi at her wedding, but she was very friendly and had also read Rachel's blog. 'I'd love to see you perform.'

As Sev and Naomi chatted about whether they could make it to Paris next month Anya's mind was on two things.

Roman, of course, and also a large bag of peanut butter and chocolate cups that Naomi had pulled out of her bag along with a silver-wrapped gift for Nadia.

'I don't think we need to bring food,' Sev said.

'Everyone loves these.' Naomi laughed. She had brought nearly a suitcase of them with her from New York and had been merrily sharing them out.

They were possibly Anya's favourite treat.

The caterer had been busy and back at the apartment champagne flowed and there were pink cupcakes and sumptuous nibbles that waiters brought out endlessly.

Anya stuck to water. She really had overdone things this week but then she watched as Naomi poured the chocolate cups she had brought from New York into a bowl and tried to resist temptation.

Libby's family were there and some other people that Anya did not know but she was only really aware of Roman.

The apartment was huge, yet she was painfully aware of his presence standing by Libby when he handed over his gift for little Nadia.

'Thank you, Roman,' Libby said. 'It's absolutely beautiful. I'm sure she will always treasure it.'

Roman nodded and when he went to get a drink, Anya could not resist asking Libby for a look at it.

She held the cross in her hand. It really was exquisite and she wondered how the hell he could afford it, then she turned and read the engraving on the back.

Strength.

Anya really needed to have strength today.

It was agony being in the same room as him, yet it was bliss to know he was there.

She was mired in confusion, for she ached to be by his side and yet she could not bring herself to go over.

A tray of food was offered and again she shook her head but her eyes kept going to the little chocolate cups that Naomi had brought.

She would have just one, she decided, and made her way over.

Anya went to open it but decided she would enjoy it later and she put it into her bag.

Maybe she could take one for the journey home, she thought, and slipped another into her bag.

Perhaps she would take a few for during the intervals so that she could remember being here with Roman today.

And then her hand stopped as she scooped another lot up and she knew that she had been seen putting the little silver chocolate cups into her bag.

Anya turned and saw Naomi frowning and then she met Roman's eyes and shame swept through her, just as it had when her mother had caught her. She had been caught again stealing food, and she did not know how to shrug it off, or to explain and, red in the face, very close to tears, she quickly walked out of the room.

'Why is Anya sneaking food?' Naomi had whispered to Sev, but Roman had heard her.

Because she had grown up having to, Roman thought, but didn't say anything.

He walked across the room and out into the hall he caught up with her.

'Leave me,' Anya said. She was desperately embarrassed and trying not to cry.

This very moment she remembered the slap of her

mother's hand on her cheek when she had been found in the cupboard cramming chocolate into her mouth. 'I'm so embarrassed.'

'No, no...' Roman said, and he opened a door to a room and pulled her inside and then straight into his arms. He held her against him. 'You don't have to be.'

'But they saw me,' Anya said. It felt horrific. She was so controlled in everything and yet she had been seen. 'They all saw me stealing food.'

'So?' He lifted her chin so that she had to look at him and Roman smiled when he so rarely did. 'You like chocolate. I'll take a bottle or two of champagne on the way out and they can talk about how rude we both are...'

His words didn't work because Anya was starting to cry.

'It's okay,' he said.

'But it's not. I just wanted some for later. I know it's stupid but I feel so awkward eating around others...'

'It's not stupid,' Roman said. 'You were sent to a cupboard to eat.'

'She always...' Anya stopped what she was about to say, not wanting to be disloyal to her mother, but Roman spoke for her.

'She always caught you,' Roman said. 'And then you would be given a slap and scolded.'

'How do you know?'

'There was no television at the orphanage,' Roman reminded her, and she gave a thin smile. 'You know I watched all that went on with you.'

And here was the one person who might properly understand because he had been there, he had seen first-hand the endless shaming whenever she had tried to get food.

'"You'll get fat," she would say.' Anya's voice shook as she recalled her mother's words. '"If you want to dance then you have—"'

'Anya,' he interrupted. 'I don't have many good things to say about your mother but, in this, Katya was doing her best to keep bringing you to work with her.' Roman told her what he had tried to on the night of their row, when she had pointed out that he knew nothing about families. 'She was trying to keep her job and keep you close to her in the evenings and not leave you at home alone.'

Anya frowned.

'The supervisor would say to her they had enough hungry mouths without feeding the staff's children. They were jealous because, as the cook, your mum could have a meal. If the supervisor had caught you eating, at best you would not have been able to come to the orphanage, at worst she would have lost her job.'

'How do you know?'

'Because I watched and I heard what went on. When I was on set-up duty for the dining room, before you came back from school, your mother would be making the dinner and she would be warned over and over that meals were not to be provided for you.'

Anya closed her eyes and thought back to those times, how her mother would send her to the cupboard to eat soup. The battle with food and her mother had started as a means to survive yet, as Anya's talent had started to shine, for Katya it had become an obsession.

For Anya now too.

Still he held her.

'Do you know,' Roman said. 'When I was growing up I always thought you were rich because you had a parent, but you were as poor as us, maybe more so—at least we were fed regularly.'

She felt better for his understanding and she thought of her mother and could see things through more forgiving eyes.

It was nice to confide in him, to be held in his arms as she recalled those times.

'I was always so hungry.'

'I know you were. Which is why, the night I took you out for dinner, I thought that a meal before your audition would be such a good idea. We had no idea about the world then.'

'They were still good times.' Anya sighed, because she had so many happy memories of back then—as children, laughing and showing off how fit she was to Daniil and Roman as they did their boxing drills. She recalled Christmas dinners when the workers' families could come in for the day. Then she would get to eat with the orphans and she would sit with the four boys rather than standing in the kitchen to watch.

'They were the best,' Roman told her.

His response was unexpected.

He held her tight into him so that she rested her head on his chest and she could hear the thump-thump of his heart.

'I didn't think that you would have any good memories of back then,' Anya said.

'I have many. For the first twelve years I had Daniil, as well as Sev and Nikolai, and I always looked forward to seeing you. Do you remember the time you brought supper to my room?'

'I wanted to kiss you,' Anya said.

'I wanted to touch your breasts,' Roman said, and she smiled.

'Did you look forward to seeing me today?' Anya asked.

'No.'

And his answer did not upset her.

She knew why.

'Because?' she breathed.

'Because of this.'

This need, this desire, this craving that only the other could satisfy.

Anya knew that if she looked up he would kiss her.

And so she looked up.

He kissed first her damp lashes, so that her eyes closed and the bliss of his kiss brought more tears. His mouth traced her cheeks and then went to her lips, where his kiss was soft, but never tentative.

She loathed his tender kisses, for they were not how things used to be and he had not learnt that from her, yet she ached for them too.

Their kiss deepened and his hands went to the thin cardigan she wore to cover her arms and slipped it off so that it dropped to the floor and his palms were now the warmth on her arms. 'Stop covering yourself,' he said.

He knew her every move.

Now he kissed her harder, a kiss that *was* familiar, and she felt herself sink into the intoxicating space that they found together. Their tongues told of the urgent quest for more and he pulled her tighter into him, and she stood on tiptoe just to feel more of him, fought not to climb onto him as she peeled her mouth from his and her direct words made him smile.

'We are not having sex in the guest room at your niece's christening.'

'Then the uncouth relations really would have arrived,' Roman said, and he smiled down at her because he had been determined to be a suave and suitable guest in Daniil's home; he just hadn't factored in having Anya there. 'If we were caught that really would give them something to talk about.'

Anya peered out from his chest and frowned. This was no guest room, Anya realised. They had been so focused on each other that they hadn't even taken in their surroundings.

'Roman!'

He looked then too and realised that they were standing in a huge room. The floors were polished wood, and it was a vast exercise area, a gymnasium that had been set up for boxing. There were mirrors, weights, punching bags. Growing up, it would have been the stuff of his and Daniil's dreams.

'No boxing ring, though,' Roman said.

For now he and Daniil fought with their demons and they fought them alone.

'One day, perhaps,' Anya said.

It was she now who soothed him. One day, perhaps he and Daniil might be able to speak properly. Libby couldn't seem to understand why Daniil and Roman were not falling over each other in joy at being finally reunited.

Anya did.

There had been so much suffering and so much self-reliance to get to this point in their lives that it was hard to admit you might want to depend on someone else, or feel worthy of their love.

'He has done so well,' Roman said. 'It is strange to see him grown up and now with a family...'

'Are you jealous of him?' Anya asked, but for her own reasons. There was something she needed to know. 'I mean, he has a wife, a new baby—'

'You don't understand twins,' Roman interrupted. 'I've never been jealous of my brother. I'm happy that he has everything I ever wanted.'

And if that was everything *Roman* had wanted, there was something she could never give him.

A baby.

His answer pained her and to avoid his eyes she walked over to a shelf set in a wall. It reminded her of her dressing table before a performance—it was like a little altar that displayed what she guessed were Daniil's most precious things. There was a photo of Daniil and Libby on their wedding day and one of Nadia too, as well as an ultrasound image. Anya knew that she was looking at something very private, and Roman, who now stood beside her, knew it too. There was a pink porcelain ornament and a few other things. Within the collection, though, there were two objects that she recognised.

'I remember these being taken,' Anya said as she took down two photos. 'Sergio brought in his camera that day.'

One image was of Daniil and Roman in boxing shorts, holding their hands up in a fighting pose.

Roman was scowling in the photo and today it made Anya smile. 'You just wanted to get the picture over and done with.'

'I did,' Roman said. 'But I am glad now that he took it.'

'Why did you give them to Daniil?'

'I didn't give them to him. I put them into his case.

I thought it might help him if he had some photos from home.'

'But that left you with none,' Anya said, and she looked at the other photo. It was of the four boys, now men, and today they were finally together again.

'We're going back to Nikolai's yacht after the party.' Roman told her what had been arranged. 'We're going to catch up on all that has gone on.'

'You're not looking forward to it?'

'I don't know,' he admitted. 'I'll tell you afterwards how it goes.'

'I shan't be here, Roman. I'm flying back to Paris this afternoon.'

'Anya, you know that we need to talk,' he said.

This week he had come to the realisation that they did. He could not be apart from her again. They were back in each other's lives.

It was Anya who resisted that now.

'No, we will fight.'

'So.' Roman shrugged. 'We know where our fights lead.'

Anya smiled but it changed midway and she shook her head.

'I don't want to know about your wife, Roman. I'm simply not ready to hear about it and I don't know if I ever shall be. I can't bear to hear about your life so I'm going back tonight and I meant what I said, I don't want to see you in Paris.'

'That's a lie.'

'In part,' Anya admitted. 'But it's also the truth.'

But Roman was having none of it. 'I have to catch up with the others but later tonight I'll have my assistant charter a plane…'

'See!' Anya said. 'Who are you? A man who gives platinum crosses with diamonds, a man who charters planes?'

'I will tell you.'

'But I can't stand to hear it,' she said.

'Wait for me?' he asked again, but she shook her head.

'I waited *so* long for you, Roman. No more.'

And then she forced herself to ask the question that she dreaded hearing the answer to.

She knew Roman. He would not stay five minutes with a person he did not like.

He had spent years with Celeste.

'Did you have feelings for her?'

Roman looked right into her eyes and he knew that to lie now would end them forever, but he was careful with his response. 'Not the same feelings that I have for you.'

'Had,' Anya corrected. 'Or you would not have stayed away.'

He said nothing.

'Did you love her?' she demanded, for he had never told her that he loved her.

He gave her the absolute truth. 'There was a kind of love that grew.'

No!

She would never be ready to hear about it.

And she couldn't bring herself to tell him the truth about babies either.

Their dreams had already been killed.

And so Anya walked off.

# CHAPTER SEVEN

ROMAN SAT IN the sky lounge of Nikolai's yacht and tried to comprehend the fact that they were together again and in such splendid surroundings.

The yacht had been docked in the Thames for two weeks and was an attraction in itself, but no one asked to be shown around and neither did Nikolai offer.

This time together was precious.

They had been apart for the best part of two decades and there was a lot to discuss in a short space of time. Out came the vodka, which was infused with ginger, and both Roman and Daniil pulled a face at the taste.

'Here.' Nikolai handed him a plain bottle and Roman poured two glasses, one for himself and the other for his twin.

'Here you go, *shishka*,' Roman said as he slid the glass over to Daniil, who shot him a black look at the use of his old nickname.

There was tension between them.

It was interesting, though, to catch up. Nikolai had always known where his life would lead—the ocean.

He had not started out in such splendour, Roman found out as they drank too much and caught up—he found out that Nikolai had at first been a stowaway on a ship.

'Anything was better than being there,' Nikolai said.

Roman nodded. He had heard back then that Nikolai had been sexually abused by a teacher and that was why he had run away.

When he'd been young, Roman remembered Nikolai building a ship out of matchsticks and he had taken it with him when he'd left. It had been found by the river.

Sev had kept it and now returned it.

'This took so long to make.' Nikolai put it down on the table and was touched that his friend had kept it all these years and had had it couriered from New York to give to him today.

'It's good you got out,' Roman said, and looked around the sky lounge. 'This would be a great place to party.'

'It is.'

'Are you seeing anyone?' Daniil asked Nikolai.

'Any *one*?' Nikolai checked, and then swiftly turned the conversation to Sev. Roman noticed the quick change of subject.

'When do you go back to New York?' Nikolai asked.

'We are flying back tonight,' Sev said. 'Daniil and Libby are coming over in late December to see in the New Year there. You two should come too.'

Daniil saw Roman's slight eye roll.

New York and happy families and more catching up he could do without for now.

His mind wandered to Anya and he was ready now to sort things out. Since seeing her again this morning he was resolute. Yes, she was doing well and at the top of her game yet there was a vulnerability in her that only he knew about.

Somehow they needed to talk and to get through those impossible conversations.

Now, though, he listened. Sev, as they had always known he would, had done well. He was brilliant and was now an expert in internet security. He had been the one who always had his head in books and yet he had also, in his own way, been the one who'd stepped up when things had got out of hand.

And they were starting to now.

Roman listened to his twin.

The family that had adopted him had proved to be awful. 'They realised their mistake by the time I arrived, I think,' Daniil explained. 'I was never going to replace their son.'

Roman found out how hard he had worked to get where he was, first in a bar of a hotel that was running into troubled times. He had found that he had an eye for numbers, Daniil explained, and in helping them out in return for shares had started to build his financial empire.

Roman sat silent. There were so many similarities between them and so many differences too, from having been separated.

'What about you, Roman?' Sev asked, a lot of vodka later.

'I left the orphanage at sixteen.' He shrugged. 'I gave boxing a go…' He looked at his brother. 'Sergio didn't know what he was talking about. I lost most fights, and I only won a few. With my winnings I got a passport and left and went to France and joined the foreign legion…' Roman did not speak of being in the secure unit of the orphanage, or the hellhole of the bedsit, and he left out the solace he had found with Anya. He could see a muscle leaping in Daniil's cheek as he spoke with brevity about the past, when the rest of the men had revealed so much more. 'I served for ten years, then I moved to Paris. And here I am.'

'Aren't you missing something out?' Daniil said. 'Aren't you going to tell us about your wife?'

Roman stared coolly at his brother and then addressed the group. 'I was married but last year Celeste died.'

Sev and Nikolai offered their condolences but Roman just responded with a brief nod. He did not know if he was worthy of them; it had not been a conventional marriage after all.

But Daniil had more to offer than sympathy. 'You came out and got married and got on with your life…' The tension that had been building since Libby had called out and he had seen his twin had Daniil rising to his feet. Roman stood and faced him as Daniil vented some of the anger he felt. 'I could have been at your wedding and there at the funeral. Instead I never even got to meet her.' Daniil was trying not to shout.

'It wasn't a marriage like you and Libby have. As Anya said, for you all to hear—I answered an advert.'

'How did Anya know?'

Roman shrugged and that incensed Daniil.

'I don't care if you answered an ad, Roman. Celeste meant something to you, for there is no way you would share your personal space with anyone who wasn't special.' He knew how dark his brother was, how deep he went, and that he had been through all this and not contacted him was infuriating.

'Daniil.' Roman was his detached best. 'You only recently changed your name…'

'Perhaps but you didn't even try to find me before then. Don't pretend now that you looked.'

'I didn't look.' Roman shrugged and then caught Daniil's fist as it was aimed at him.

'Do you want me to give you matching cheeks?' Roman warned.

'Enough,' Sev said—he was always the one who had stepped in when things escalated.

Both men agreed.

Enough anger for now.

'I just want to know all that has happened,' Daniil said, and they shared a brief embrace, though it was more like a boxing clinch.

'One day, perhaps,' Roman answered, borrowing the words Anya had used when they had stumbled on Daniil's gym.

He wanted to tell them more but the conversation about his marriage belonged first with Anya.

So, for now they sat and exchanged phone numbers and Daniil forwarded the ones he now had to Roman.

Within them was Anya's number.

They briefly met each other's eyes.

Daniil knew there was something going on between Roman and Anya.

With twins who had once been so close, there were times when no words were needed and they shared a smile so subtle that, even if they had been looking, the others would have missed it.

It was time to go. They were all a bit worse for wear and Nikolai saw them off his yacht and they stepped out into the night.

They all shook hands and then Sev headed off to return to his honeymoon and that left just Roman and Daniil standing on the quay.

Roman saw a certain redhead—Rachel—sitting on a

seat, and knew now the reason for Nikolai's evasive answer about women, but he did not let on to Daniil.

'Where are you staying?' Daniil asked.

Roman told him the name of the hotel he had checked into.

'Come and stay with us.'

Roman shook his head. They were nowhere near ready for that. 'You have a new baby.'

'She's your niece. I don't want you in a hotel when I have a home.'

'No, I want to go back to my own apartment. I don't really know why,' Roman admitted. He wasn't being rude in not accepting the invitation and he tried to let his brother know that. 'I am just sick of the hotel, even though it is very nice. I just want…' He couldn't really explain that he wanted to be amongst his own things and to sleep in his own bed. 'The hotel has everything…' It was luxurious indeed. 'I would just like to be amongst my own things.'

'You're homesick,' Daniil said.

There was a word for those feelings, Roman found out.

He was homesick not just for his home but for Paris, because Anya was there.

They said good night and as Roman walked off he took out his phone.

He called his assistant to arrange his flight and headed straight for the airport. As he sat on the tarmac, staring out at the navy London sky, he took out his phone and called Anya.

She picked up her phone without thinking. She had assumed it was Mika to see if she was ready, or one of the others, as they had agreed to meet in the foyer and she was running a little bit late.

She almost dropped the phone when she realised it was Roman.

'How did you get my number?' she asked.

'It doesn't matter. Where are you?'

'We're just about to head out for supper.'

'We?'

'It is not your business,' Anya coolly answered.

'Pack up your things. I'll be there in the next couple of hours…'

'Excuse me?'

'You heard.' And now he used Daniil's line. 'You're not staying in a hotel when I have a home…'

The difference with Anya was they *were* ready for that.

Roman was sure.

They were ready to explore the past together and see where that left them.

'You wouldn't have said that last time I was here,' Anya retorted. 'You were too busy being a mail-order—'

'Anya,' Roman broke in. 'We shall speak about Celeste when you can manage to say her name without venom.'

'Never,' Anya said.

'Then we shall speak about why I left.'

'You left because you could not stand to see me succeed.' That was how she had justified it in the end, but she could almost see the flick of his wrist as he dismissed the thoughts that she had built like a scaffold to protect her bruised heart.

'Rubbish.'

'Were you so intimidated—?'

'You don't intimidate me,' he broke in.

That alone almost brought her to tears. Everyone else was intimidated by her, everyone thought her cold and unfeeling. Roman, though, saw through it. He knew the heart behind the ice. He had known her passion and her hopes and fears.

'I would have loved to have been beside you when you soared,' Roman said.

He wanted to be by her side now; he felt ready to be and would do whatever it took.

'No!' Anya shook her head. 'You wanted to make your riches and refused to be poor with me.'

It had been *such* a poor life.

People assumed wealth yet dancers danced for the love of it. She had been cocooned and enclosed in a world where few made any real money. For Anya that had only happened in recent years. She was no prodigy, she had had to fight and to work harder and smarter to get to where she was. Only now had she paid off the debts she had accumulated. Before that she had lived in a tiny flat that she'd shared with her mother—her climb to the top had been rough indeed.

Now she would spend the next decade, or however long her body gave her, securing her future for when dancing was gone.

Right now she had a performance that she needed to focus on, but Roman had other ideas.

'Pack your case, then text me the name of your hotel.'

'No.'

'I mean it, Anya. I shall tear up Paris tonight to find you.'

'Good luck with the gendarmes, then. Don't call me again, Roman.'

She ended the call and turned her phone off.

Then she thought about turning it on to delete his number but knew she could not bear to do that.

There was temptation in her bag, all the way through a late supper with the sponsors. Not just the chocolate cups but Roman's number on her phone.

All she could think of was him and his call to take her to his home.

And she thought about the last time they had shared a bed.

Or rather a mattress.

She thought about their first time and the eventual love that they had made.

He had been so cold and oblivious to the pleasure of touch at first.

So wanting to get things over and done with.

And then they had stumbled into intense pleasure and had made memories that nothing could ever erase.

As the jet carried him closer to Anya, Roman stared out of the window…and remembered the same.

# CHAPTER EIGHT

ANYA CAME OUT of the stage door and into the side alley and was ready to run home, not just to get out of the freezing snow but also because she had news for her mother. She had just been told that she would be auditioning in two weeks' time for a part in the *corps de ballet* for the next performance.

It was the step up from apprenticeship and she had worked so hard for it.

And then she saw him.

Roman Zverev.

She had not seen him since he had left the orphanage a couple of years ago but she had heard about him.

He was wearing torn black jeans and a thin jacket and his black hair was long and damp as it gathered snow. He was walking towards her.

'You lost your fight,' Anya said by way of greeting, and looked at his bruised eye and cheek and swollen mouth.

'Good news travels fast.'

He looked at Anya. She had always been perfection to him, so delicate and yet so strong. The only thing he had missed about the orphanage was her and now her pale green eyes met his, but this time without the scold of her mother to haul them from his gaze.

The years since Daniil had left had been hell and she had been the only balm.

Sergio had continued to attempt to channel his anger into boxing but it was as if the desire in Roman to be a boxer had left with his twin and he had won only a handful of fights.

Last night he had lost to a brute who had been a lot bigger than him.

'You were in the wrong weight category,' Anya said. 'You need to lose weight before weigh-in—your opponent would have. You could have scraped in as a mid-lightweight. Instead you faced a man who just scraped into middleweight.'

She was an athlete, a dancer, and knew all about nutrition as well as starving and muscle definition.

'Sergio is out of touch—' she continued but Roman broke in.

'I don't need dieting advice from you, Anya.'

He didn't. She was tiny and far thinner than he remembered her to be, and that concerned him.

Yet she was even more beautiful.

'Anyway...' Roman shrugged '...I'm sick of boxing. I've applied for a passport.'

'Why?'

'Because there is nothing for me here.'

'Are you going to look for Daniil?'

'No.' He shook his head. 'I'm not turning up on his doorstep...'

'He might want you to.'

'No.' Roman was adamant. He would not be a burden on his brother.

'So where will you go?'

Wherever it was, Anya didn't want him to leave. Even

though she hadn't seen him in two years, she liked knowing that he was around and hearing about him sometimes. She had dreamed of a moment like this, meeting him on the street, and now it had transpired.

'What have you been up to?' he asked.

'Just my dance,' Anya said. 'I just found out that I have an audition in two weeks' time for a place in the *corps de ballet*.'

He just stared.

'A part in their next performance,' she explained. 'Just a small part but I would be on the stage.'

'You'll get it,' Roman said. He had always known that she would go far.

'Would you come and see me perform if I did?'

Roman looked up at the theatre she had just come out of and could not imagine himself inside there, and yet he wanted to see her perform.

'Yes.'

He didn't know how, just that one day he would.

His answer meant everything to Anya and she reached out to touch the bruise over his eye but he moved his head back in reflex.

The only touches he knew were punches, jabs...

There had been zero affection in his life.

None.

Ever.

The girls who hung around the boxing gym adored Roman and did not care if he was not affectionate with them or that he didn't want affection back.

But then her fingers met his skin and she lightly stroked the swollen flesh and she watched his eyes close.

Anya had always had a thing for him.

'No boys,' her mother said. 'To dance, there must be sacrifice.'

There had been *so* many sacrifices, but Roman was her guilty pleasure and she had touched herself many times while thinking of him.

After the fight with his brother, Roman's file had been marked Unsuitable for Adoption and he had been sent to the secure wing, though Anya knew he had not needed to be held there.

At sixteen he had left the orphanage and for two years she had missed him very much.

Now she could see his lips and that bruised, swollen mouth she wanted to taste. Her breathing was coming in a strange rhythm, as if she had just completed floor exercise, and yet she was standing still.

His breathing was slower and deeper, though, almost as it was before a fight, pulling oxygen into every cell, in preparation, anticipation.

Who kissed who?

Neither knew.

Their mouths simply met.

And it was soft for a second, but he could take pain so he pressed her into deeper contact and his tongue slipped into her mouth.

With one taste she was his. Both had waited for this moment for so long. Her arms went up and her hand met the back of his head, and then her shoulders met the wall.

He kissed her harder and she felt him unbuttoning her jacket and then the warmth of his hands as he touched her breast through her jumper as he had wanted to for so long.

Anya loved the intimate contact. The mingling of tongues continued and now her hand was busy. She reached down just so she could feel what had been pressing into her, and it was thick and hard.

They were dirty deep kissing down an alley and all thought of telling her mother about her audition was gone but then his hand caught her wrist and pulled it away from where she wanted to linger.

'Anya...'

'I want you, Roman, I always have. Take me back to yours,' she said. 'Take me.'

'You need to go home,' he said, breathing more rapidly now. He was ashamed of where he lived. 'Go back to your mother...' He walked off and she watched him go, yet despite the cold snow her mouth and body were on fire from her first kiss and she would not leave things there.

She ran.

Down the alleyway she ran and leapt onto his back and clung to him like a monkey, and though Roman carried on walking he laughed.

He laughed.

But then he swung her around so her legs wrapped around his waist and they faced the other, and as he walked on she asked him a question that she had asked a couple of years ago on that night when she had taken his supper to him.

'How did you get the chocolate?'

He hadn't answered then, they had just stared at each other and turned each other on in their first moment alone.

Now he told her.

'Sev. He won a medal and they gave it to him. He saved it for me.'

'You should have had it.'

'I always wanted to have something I could give you,' Roman said, and now he had a question for her.

'What did your mother say when she caught you? We had to go back to our rooms and I just saw her going to the cupboard and then the shouts.'

'She said you were trouble.' Anya smiled. 'That you were a saboteur.'

Roman stopped walking and he tried to peel her from him but she refused to be put down.

'Anya...' He did not know how best to voice it but that word had stung for it was his fear that he might sabotage not just Anya but his brother, were he to go looking for him. For years he had been told he was bad news, trouble, and that no family would ever want him to be a part of theirs.

And when he could not properly explain, they kissed again, her sex against his flat stomach and his erection stretching to reach it, and they both knew where this would lead. It was February tomorrow, and that meant that, although it was only four o'clock, soon it would be starting to get dark. 'You should go home.'

'I want to be with you, though,' she said. 'I want you to be my first. It has to be you.'

And Roman could not stand the thought of it being anyone other than him.

'Take me to your home,' Anya said.

'It's not a home.'

It was a bedsit in a building that the government provided for troubled young men like him.

'We make it a home,' Anya said, and they kissed in the cold, yet she felt warm for her feet were not on the ground, her legs were wrapped around him and her body pressed to his as their mouths generated heat.

He lowered her to the ground and they walked out onto the street. The snow was cold but she didn't notice it with his arm around her, but outside a pharmacy he told her to wait outside.

They walked again, yet he stopped at another store.

'What are you doing?'

'Just wait here,' he said, and she wrapped her arms around herself in an attempt to stay warm. Finally he came out, carrying a bag, and she asked what was in it.

'Never mind.'

They walked further until they came to the large grey house where Roman had a bedsit.

They dropped contact. He walked ahead of her and she followed him up a set of stairs. He took out a key and opened a door but again she was told to wait outside.

'Roman?'

Anya did not like this house and knew there could be trouble but she waited nervously, wondering what the hell he was up to.

The door opened a moment later and she stepped in and though she did not acknowledge to Roman that she knew, she saw that on the mattress on the floor were new sheets and a fresh pillowcase.

It had taken just a moment for him to make up the mattress. After all, he had spent his life rising early and making his bed, but that he had done what he could to make this room as pleasing as possible for her meant everything to Anya.

Alone in his room they weren't shy, perhaps just a little awkward at first.

It was almost as cold in the room as it was outside and Roman fed coins into a meter and a small heater came on, but it would take ages to heat the room.

'Get undressed,' he said.

Perhaps not romantic but as Anya took off her clothes he put them on a chair by the heater so they would be warm when she dressed.

From her time in changing rooms Anya was very comfortable dressing and undressing in front of others but now she could feel his eyes on her body and it made her blush, though not in embarrassment.

Shivering, she got onto the mattress and slipped under the starchy sheet and watched as he now undressed. She was glad there was no curtain on the small window. A dusky grey wintery sky above allowed her to see his body as he peeled off his jumper.

He was magnificent. Broad and muscular and, though she was used to toned bodies, his was absolute bliss. There were black and purple bruises on his chest from his fight yesterday, and the paleness of his skin made her hand want to reach out.

He retrieved the condoms he had bought and tossed them down to the floor by the mattress then pulled down black jeans and his underwear. Anya felt her breath burn in her lungs at the sight of him. The thought of that inside her made her feel nervous and excited. As he came over and got onto the low mattress it was only the cold that kept her under the sheet, but he peeled it off and would keep her warm with his skin.

She felt his arms and wanted them to be wrapped around her and she ran her hand over his thigh, just enjoying the strength of him and that finally they could touch and hold each other.

He reached over for the condoms.

'Roman...' Anya said. 'Kiss me first.'

He kissed her again, and it was deeper than last time,

rougher than in the alley, and she tried to slow him down with her tongue. His hands played with her small breasts and he moaned into her mouth.

'Taste them,' Anya begged.

He did and he licked and sucked so hard that it caused the most delicious of hurts. She could feel him hard against her thigh and then again his hands patted outside the mattress for the condoms.

'Wait,' Anya said, because she wanted more of his mouth.

'I don't want to wait,' he said, and he rolled onto his back, annoyed at the tease as Anya climbed on and sat on his stomach,

He did not like the kisses that trailed over his chest, and the nip of her teeth on his nipples, or rather he did but he did not want to feel her wet sex on his stomach when he wanted to be inside.

'I want to come,' he said, and she lifted and knelt, but instead of lowering herself onto his hard length she sat on his thighs and took his erection in her hand and started to stroke him.

'I can do that myself.'

She was too slow, too tender and she watched his sulky face as she stroked him.

'We'd be finished by now if I'd left it to you,' she said.

'I want to be finished.' Roman had grown up used to a very quick come in the shower, and even now that was his preferred place.

Sex he liked hard and fast. Where was the pleasure in lying back, watching someone stroke him?

'You're too slow.'

'Do it yourself then,' she said, and got off. Then she decided to do something that he could not do for himself and knelt aside him. She heard his raw moan as she tasted him, as she licked his head and then slid her mouth down and sucked him.

'More...' he moaned.

And more Anya gave. She licked and sucked and loved the pressure he exerted with his hand to her head and the way his voice told her to go harder, take him deeper.

He held her hair and thrust into her and Anya wanted to touch herself because she was so close to coming.

Then she felt him swell and a powerful rush into her mouth and she tasted his salt and heard his ragged breathing as he lay there with his eyes closed.

And when he opened them Roman could not see her at first, for she was lying down, her head by his feet.

'My turn now.'

He knelt up and hauled her over, parted her legs and looked down at her.

'You're beautiful, Anya,' he said, and his fingers explored her intimate lips.

She propped herself up on her elbows and looked down. 'When I touch myself to you...' she pointed '...I touch there.'

He was hardening again, from looking at her and thinking of Anya touching herself to him.

And her finger showed him the little bud and then his hand swept her finger away and he lowered his head.

Her sob told him he hit exactly the right location, so he sucked her there and then blew and sucked and licked till it was Anya who swore, and who pleaded for more.

He parted her thighs further and he was still rough but now expert. His unshaven jaw felt delicious, the probe of his tongue so sublime that not even her elbows could hold her and she went onto her back and arched up.

She started to moan, he told her to hush, but he said it into her sex. Anya gritted her teeth and tried to hold onto the scream and as she did, the tension released to his mouth, his lips thrummed to the pulse of her and then Roman lowered her hips.

Anya felt spent. Her thighs were together and her hand covered her sex as it ached yet she was high on arousal and he moved so that he was over her body and on his elbows, looking down.

'I don't want to hurt you,' he said.

'I want you to,' she said, and she peeled her hand away and his muscled thigh parted her legs.

He held onto himself as if holding himself back and then he entered a little. His face was beside hers and he heard her sob and he pulled back.

He tried again and it hurt so much she let out a cry of pain. 'Just do it,' she said.

'Anya?'

'Please.'

He did so and it killed her. The tear and stretch as he filled her was a heated agony and the feel as he hit her cervix was so bruising that she felt sick, and then she opened her eyes and he was deep inside her.

He kissed her in a way that he had not before. It started as an apology, then a kiss to chase away the pain. This was a kiss she wanted, tender, breathless, and as he started to move inside her the pain was replaced by warmth and she soon found she was moving with him.

For Roman the feel of their aroused skin sliding together felt sublime. It was like first contact, real contact with another soul. The touch of her hands on his shoulders he welcomed and then the roaming of them over his buttocks drew him further in.

They rolled to their sides to face each other and kiss deeply and then watch for a moment.

He thrust harder and watched as he did so. Her blood was on him and he would never hurt her again.

'Roman...' There was an urgent plea in her husky voice.

Anya had come to the thought of him many times, but never like this, for it was moving through her slowly. She felt as if she were dying a delicious death as she lost contact with all her senses, apart from the one that was him.

He turned her again, she was on her back again and he was heavy on top of her and it felt sublime.

Then she came hard; sweet and hot, it just flooded her body and gathered at her centre. And it beckoned him to fill her. Which he did. His rapid thrusts were deliciously jarring, and then the rush of him inside her was heaven. Anya's orgasm dragged back and then in like the ocean and swept them together to a place neither had ever been.

They lay still.

It was dark yet their bodies felt light and the heater had now warmed the room.

'I don't want to go home,' she said as she lay in bliss.

'You have to.'

'I want to be with you,' she said, and she turned to him. 'I love you.'

He stared back at her and then rose from the mattress. 'Come on, you need to get home.'

He dressed her in warm clothes and then walked her through the snow back to her world.

A world she didn't want to be in without him.

* * *

Even the memory of them made Anya hungry.

She sat in a restaurant in Paris and usually she would toy with a quail-egg salad and pick out the croutons.

Tonight she ate quail.

But not even a generous supper could dim the hunger, for it was Roman she craved.

She turned on her phone at the end of the meal.

He had not called her again and that made her frown for she had expected more persistence.

More thrill from his chase.

The troupe wandered back towards the hotel. There were posters up, advertising the ballet, and there was a buzz that the famed dance company had now arrived in Paris. There were a couple of media journalists outside so Mika slipped an arm around her.

'Can you do me a favour?' Anya asked him.

'I can.' Mika frowned in surprise. It was most unlike Anya to ask for anything.

'Would you look after my phone tonight and not give it back to me, even if I beg you to?'

'Can I ask why?'

She never told anyone what was going on in her life but Anya could not stand to be alone in her head any more with this.

She needed friends.

'Because the love of my life now has my number, and I have his and I am scared that I shall be too weak not to use it when I need him tonight.'

And Mika, who had a formidable reputation with woman but had secretly loved Anya for years, had his heart broken right there and then.

'Of course,' he said, and took her phone.

They walked in through the sumptuous foyer, and Mika dropped his arm and abruptly went to walk off.

'Where are you going?' she asked. She had hoped for conversation, to share her pain with another soul who might help her to understand.

'To the bar.'

As opposed to the barre.

And then she felt it. Just as she had when she had stolen the chocolate cups—as she stood there she knew that she was being watched.

She turned and there Roman was, sitting in the sumptuous foyer, his legs outstretched, utterly relaxed and clearly waiting for her to arrive. He had that glint of triumph in his eyes as he stood.

She felt the sudden impulse to run, to get away from him, yet her body disobeyed that command, which meant that she just stood there, loaded with adrenaline, as he calmly walked towards her.

'How?' Anya could manage but one word.

How had he found her?

# CHAPTER NINE

'YOU HAVE TWO CHOICES,' Roman said, without answering her question. 'We go up to your suite so that you can pack, or I take you to my home now and send someone to collect your things.'

'I have told you, I don't want to go to your home. I need to rehearse. I need—'

'This isn't a debate,' he told her. 'You are coming back with me.'

'You can't make me,' Anya said. 'I'll have security remove you!'

'Why would they remove a guest from the hotel?'

'You've checked in here?'

'Of course,' he said. 'And, really, Anya, do you think they could remove me?'

He looked to the entrance and Anya's gaze followed and, sure enough, the two security guards, dealing with the press, would be no match for Roman.

'I'll put you over my shoulder now,' he warned.

He would.

'Or,' Roman said, as he took her bag from her and opened it, taking out the hotel card and checking her room number, 'we can go up now and get your things.'

'I'm not…'Anya started, but he had already taken her by the elbow and marched her towards the elevator.

'How?' she asked again as Roman pressed a button that would take them to her floor. 'I told Reception that no information was to be given out.'

'I didn't call Reception.'

'Did you have me followed?' she asked, her voice rising.

'You're too dramatic,' he said as the doors opened and they stepped out onto her floor.

She always had been.

Until the day he had left, she had been upfront with her emotions and had expressed them. She had been closed off for years but he had flicked the switch and turned her back to the woman she had been when he'd last been in her life.

'I want to know how you found me.'

'Your boyfriend put a picture up on social media of the view from his hotel room. I know the skyline,' Roman said, and then she heard the edge to his voice as he asked a question. 'Are you sharing a room with him? Is that why you don't want me here?'

She was not ready for this, Anya thought. She was not ready to reveal the depth of her love—that there had been no one since him, that there could never be anyone other than him. Neither was she ready to hear about his wife, and suddenly the instinct to run that had hit her in the foyer kicked in now.

She turned and ran back towards the lifts.

Roman did as he'd promised.

He caught up easily, picked her up and threw her over his shoulder.

'Put me down.'

He did not do as asked and she beat at his back.

'I thought that you liked to be lifted…' Roman said as he strode back down the corridor, and then he thought of Mika holding her. 'Does he do this…?'

He ran a hand up between her legs.

She smiled unseen at the jealous edge to Roman's voice as they arrived at the door to her suite.

'He does,' Anya said, 'only with far more skilled hands.' She felt the grip of his fingers tighten high on her thigh and then his hand moved and he fingered her damp knickers, where she was hot and swollen for him.

'Liar,' he said, for there were no more skilled hands than his where Anya was concerned.

He removed his hand and swiped the card, pushed open the door and strode through. He dropped her onto the bed and she lay staring up at him.

She was breathless.

So too was he.

Not from exertion. He had hiked through rugged terrain with far more weight than Anya on his back.

He stared down at her and there was a dangerous edge to the air. She felt he might take her now, might get on the bed and simply have her.

And she fought the desire for just that.

Then suddenly he turned and walked away.

He went into the bathroom and stood for a moment holding the sink, looking at the marble bench where he saw just her toothbrush, her things. Relief washed over him when he saw that she did not share her suite with Mika.

He understood Anya better now, how she could not bear to discuss Celeste, for Roman knew he had serious work ahead of him. Jealousy and possession churned the bile in his stomach and he took a long drink of water.

Anya worked with Mika, she trained with Mika and would perform with him. Roman knew that if he and Anya were to have any chance at being together then he would have to learn how to deal with that.

In the midst of reclaiming them, he had to acknowledge and accept her past, her present, and for that reason he stood for a moment to regroup.

Anya lay there. She couldn't see him, she just lay there trying to work out what to do next.

Roman came out and offered a solution.

'We need to get to know each other again,' he said.

She was scared to see his home, scared to get more involved in his life—after all he had left her so easily last time. Their love had burned just as intensely then and yet he had walked away.

And he had married *her*!

'I know you already, Roman,' Anya said. She did. She knew his heart for it had connected with hers many years ago. She knew the might of the pain he could cause, had caused, and still did. 'I can't forgive you.'

'I'm not asking for you to forgive me,' Roman said. 'But we need some time together to at least—'

'No.'

'There will be no discussion about Celeste until you are ready.'

Anya closed her eyes even at the sound of his wife's name.

'We will just spend some time together, catching up, little by little…'

'Why?'

'Because we are back in each other's lives.' It was why he had stayed away for so long.

'I need to focus on my dance,' Anya said. It wasn't going well. Since Roman had come back she had been rehearsing less and eating more. 'I have to rehearse and train every day.'

'Of course you can rehearse and train. I'm not kidnapping you.'

She looked into coal-black eyes as he spoke.

'I want you to come back to my home and I know that you want to be there too.'

'I don't want to share a bed with you.'

'Of course you do.' Roman said it as fact. It was. 'But if you want to play coy then you can stay in one of the guest rooms.'

'Guest rooms?'

Who was this man? Anya thought. Maybe she didn't know him after all. 'I don't think—'

'Don't think,' he interrupted, and he went to the wardrobe and took out her cases.

She lay and watched as he made a call to someone and spoke in French then he calmly packed up her things.

Calmly, because it felt right.

Roman was taking her home.

# CHAPTER TEN

ANYA GOT INTO the car as her cases were loaded.

She had insisted on not checking out of the hotel. It felt safer knowing she had a bolt hole to return to at any time if they didn't work out.

And she very much doubted that they could, for she simply could not foresee a time when they could speak of Celeste, and neither could she ever forgive him for leaving her all those years ago.

He had ended their relationship without consultation.

And now, with just as little consultation, he was starting it again.

Roman had a driver.

Oh, her heart knew him, but who was this man and how had he got to where he was? Her brain was dizzy from him.

'I'm tired, Roman,' she said as he got into the car and sat beside her.

It was long after midnight and she was utterly drained.

'I know,' he replied. 'Soon you can rest.'

His apartment wasn't very far from the hotel she was staying at.

He lived in the chic Eighth District just off the Avenue des Champs-Élysées, which was arguably the most beautiful avenue in the world.

How?

He insisted his money was his own but Anya knew where he had come from and it did not seem possible to her. As they drove through heavy gates and into a private street a horrible thought occurred. They pulled up at a stunning classic Parisian residence and there was one thing Anya had to know before she got out of the car.

'Is this where you lived with her?'

'No,' Roman answered. 'I bought this last year.'

And so she got out.

The foyer was serviced and they were greeted. The gates of an antique elevator opened and an elderly man came out and spoke for a moment with Roman in French.

There were several elevators and it was like a faded, luxurious hotel, Anya thought.

'This is the only elevator you can use. I shall give you a key,' Roman explained as they stepped in. 'If you press this…' he showed her which button '…it takes you straight up to my apartment.'

It made no sense.

Still, she asked no questions, just nodded as they jolted upwards. When the lift came to a halt he pulled the door open and she stepped into luxury that wasn't faded, but magnificent.

They stood in a reception area the walls of which were deep crimson; the ceiling and carpets were too. There were antique furnishings and a huge gilded mirror in which Anya could see her pale reflection.

An elderly rotund woman came through and conversed in rapid French with Roman before speaking directly to Anya, who shook her head to say she didn't understand.

She was almost too tired even to speak.

'Josie said that your room is ready and asked if you would like some supper.'

'Tell her, no, thank you,' Anya said.

'Do you speak any French?' he asked.

'I know an awful lot of ballet terms,' she said, 'but that's about it.'

The elderly man returned at that moment and deposited the cases, presumably in her room, and when he came out he and Josie wished Roman and herself good night and Anya waited as they spoke for a few moments.

She was more than a little bewildered.

Roman chatted easily with them and whatever he had just said had made Josie laugh.

They did not seem like staff and yet they were here in the dead of the night, sorting out his home, dealing with his sudden guest, and now they were leaving in the internal elevator.

'Who *are* they?' Anya said.

'Josie and Claude,' Roman explained, and now even he laughed and it was a rare sound. In fact, she hadn't heard that sound since they had met again. It was low, deep and familiar from times gone by and she wanted to hear it again.

'They came with the apartment,' Roman explained as he showed her through to perhaps the most beautiful lounge ever. Heavy jade silk drapes were closed and the large living room was gently lit by damask-shaded lamps. Anya looked up at the high ceiling and the large chandelier, which, though opulent, was somehow soothing.

'I didn't know about them,' Roman explained further. 'The first morning I woke up here, I came through to the kitchen and there Josie was, making breakfast.

*"Bonjour, monsieur,"* she said, and then told me that she would bring my food out to me on the balcony. I went out there and there was Claude, setting up. I was as confused as you are now,' he said, and it made her smile. 'All I could think was that I was glad that I hadn't been armed at the time!'

Now it was Anya who laughed.

'It turns out that they have a small apartment downstairs, and take care of this one. They've been here for decades. You'll get used to them.'

'Did you?'

'It took a while,' Roman admitted.

Could *they* last a while? Anya wondered. Could they somehow be together while avoiding the hurtful things that needed to be discussed?

'Do you want me to show you around?' he offered, but she shook her head.

'Not now, I'm really tired.'

'Then I'll show you where you are sleeping.'

True to his word, he did not try to persuade her to share his bed and Anya found that she was pouting as he showed her the door and then wished her good night. He walked off without so much as a kiss.

She stepped in and again the décor was amazing. The room was as big as her entire apartment. The wallpaper was a riot of pinks and reds and the drapes were the same design but in silk. A canopied bed was dressed beautifully and on the intricate bedside table Josie had placed a glass and a jug covered with a weighted circle of linen.

It really was stunning. There was even a reading area, with a dark chaise longue and bookshelves that were overflowing. The books were all in French, though.

Anya couldn't resist so she pulled open the drapes and the shutters and there was the Eiffel Tower twinkling in the night.

It was the most romantic, feminine room Anya had ever been in and she would never have expected it to be in a home that Roman owned.

She undressed in a pretty bathroom and pulled on a slip nightdress.

It was a home that felt like a palace, Anya thought as she climbed into the very high bed.

She had been living in hotels for weeks and now she lay staring out at the view, trying to take in the fact that she was there.

There were too many questions that buzzed in her mind.

Though exhausted, she could not relax. Though aching with tiredness, she could not sleep.

She could not lie down a hallway away from Roman.

She could hear him turning off lights and she knew that he had gone to bed.

She ate one of her chocolate cups.

And then another.

But that was not where her hunger had originated. She climbed out of bed and her feet dropped silently to the floor. Like a homing pigeon she walked down the long hall and turned to the left.

There was a high door and a shaft of light was coming from beneath it. She knew he was in there and she opened it.

He sat on the bed, his head in his hands almost in grief, and though he spoke he did not turn towards her.

'Go to bed, Anya.'

She did not.

She stayed.

He had taken off his shirt and was wearing only black trousers. Every inch of his body Anya had thought she had known, yet the livid scars on his back proved her knowledge of Roman to be flawed. She let out a small cry and it seared through him.

He did not want her to see them, for he knew they would cause her pain and yet there was this odd relief that she knew now.

She climbed onto the bed and touched his back. 'What happened?'

'Just leave it for now.'

'You could have died and I would never have known!' she sobbed, and he just sat with his head in his hands as he remembered how close he had come to just that as Anya spoke on, her anger and desperation evident in every word. 'I waited for you, and I feared for you,' she wept, and everything she was trying to hold back from admitting started to pour out. 'I was scared for you in war zones and I grieved in case you lay dead. And yet I hoped and prayed that you were safe and that one day you would come for me, and while I did all that, you took *her* as your wife.'

He stood and for the second time that night he picked her up and put her over his shoulder. She kissed the scars on his back as he carried her back to her room. 'I don't want to play coy,' Anya pleaded. 'I want your bed.'

'When we are capable of an adult discussion about Celeste and...' Roman too was not ready, he could not even say Mika's name. He pulled back the covers that were littered with the foil of her chocolate cups and popped her in. 'We can reward ourselves later.'

'I'll *never* be able to speak of it nicely.'

'Then you'll never get your reward.'

'Oh, so you're on a sex strike?' she scoffed. 'We'll soon see who gives in first.'

'You don't know the life I have lived,' Roman said. 'Believe me, I know how to go without.'

He did not walk out but closed the shutters and drapes and then came and sat on the bed.

'It is too beautiful not to look at,' he said of the Eiffel Tower. 'You need to sleep.'

'I have class at eight.'

'That's not long from now.'

She looked at his shoulder and it too was scarred, and she put her hand up to it.

'Tell me.'

'Shrapnel.'

'How bad was it?' she asked.

'It was fairly bad,' he said. 'I had a punctured lung.'

'Could you have died?'

He nodded.

And she wanted to ask if he'd thought of her then, but Roman was so honest that she was scared to ask, in case she did not like the answer.

'My comrade was worse, though,' Roman said, and her hand remained on his shoulder, feeling the muscle and the ridges of the scars. 'I tried to keep him conscious.'

And he told her how Dario had spoken of the stock market and the rules to which he had been unable to adhere.

'I could, though,' he said. And he told her about his rehabilitation in Provence. 'I was going to come out of the legion after five years, but they were good to me there and when my contract came around again I felt it right to serve for another five years.'

He told her how he had started to make his money, and then she believed that it was all his own.

'Your comrade?'

'Dario,' Roman said. 'He is still in the legion.'

'Do you keep in touch with him?'

'I do,' he said.

He turned off the light, gave her a brief kiss on the lips and then left. She lay in the dark, and slept. A sleep so deep that when she awoke Anya took a moment to realise where she was.

The previous night's events felt like a dream.

She went into her bag for her phone to find out the time, but remembered that Mika had it. She went into the bathroom and freshened up.

Did she dress for breakfast?

Was it even breakfast time?

She pulled on her robe and hurried out. She had class at eight and then rehearsals.

*'Bonjour, mademoiselle,'* Josie called out.

*'Bonjour, madame,'* Anya called back, and then wandered out to the balcony where Roman sat, reading the newspaper.

Actually, he lounged in a chair.

He was wearing only black jeans and he hadn't shaved and when he looked up and gave her a smile, Anya had to fight not to go and sit on his lap and kiss him.

'What time is it?' she asked.

'It is almost seven, I was going to get you up then,' Roman said as she took a seat at the breakfast table. There were flowers in a vase and baguettes and pastries and a large silver jug, presumably coffee.

'How did you sleep?' Anya asked him.

'I always sleep well,' he told her. 'So you don't have to ask. If that changes I'll let you know. What about you?'

'I never sleep well,' she answered. 'But I did in the end. My room's beautiful. You didn't choose the furnishings, I take it?'

Roman shook his head. 'The apartment came as it was, even the staff! That was one of the most appealing things about it. I would have had no idea how to decorate it.'

'Well, it's perfect,' Anya said, and reached for the coffee pot to fill her cup, and then frowned when delectable hot chocolate poured out.

'I would like green tea,' she said, cross with him for the temptation.

'Sure,' Roman said, and went to call out to Josie, but she was already there, bringing out some yoghurt and fresh berries, which she added to the collection of food on the table as Roman put in Anya's order.

'It might be a while,' Roman said when Josie left. 'She will have to go to the shop to get some.'

'Oolong tea, then, or just—'

'Do I look like a man who keeps a herbal tea collection?' Roman interrupted.

'I'm sure you've had other lovers ask for green tea,' she sneered.

'I don't bring women here,' Roman said. 'There are hotels for all that.'

And he both hurt her with the knowledge that, yes, there were women, and comforted her that he never bought them here, and yet here she was.

'Tell Josie not to bother,' she grumbled, and shot him a look as she poured hot chocolate. 'Are you trying to fatten me up again?'

'Anya,' Roman said calmly, 'I asked Josie to provide

an alternative breakfast for you.' He sliced open a baguette and slathered it with butter. 'I drank black tea in the orphanage and then black coffee in the legion—' he left out the years they could not speak of '—and then, that morning, when I found Josie in my kitchen, she brought out the same breakfast as she did for me today. She gets up early and goes to the bakery and she buys fresh bread and pastries and then comes back and makes the hot chocolate. I like it. That's it. My choice of breakfast has nothing to do with you. You shall have a full herbal tea selection by the time you get back from dance.'

'I might be back late. I have to work hard these next weeks,' Anya said as she reached for berries and yoghurt but she did have hot chocolate.

'Come back whenever it suits,' he said to the newspaper but then he looked up. 'Just come back.'

'We've never had breakfast together,' she said.

'No,' he agreed, and put down his paper and looked at her. 'We cannot linger, though, you don't want to be late.'

Maybe they had changed.

In their two weeks together they would make love in the morning and Anya would forget the time and arrive late for class. Afterwards, when usually she would stay late and rehearse further, she would race back to his.

Her mother had once been at the stage door and had demanded that she come home and had chased her. Anya had outrun her, just for another night in Roman's arms.

'I won't get in the way of your dance again,' he said.

He had learnt his lesson.

After the disastrous meal and the row afterwards, the audition hadn't gone well. Anya hadn't made the corps and Katya had sought him out and come into the gym where he'd been training for his next fight. Anya had talent, she had told him. Anya had been doing well until he had arrived back on the scene.

'You sabotage her dance,' Katya had spat at him, and it was then she had told Roman that he was a burden to the system and that no family would want him in theirs. 'You bring her down to your low level. Now I have to comfort her as she cries. All the work she has put in, all the agony she went through and now she has not made the corps. I wish, how I wish, for Anya's sake, that you had never existed.'

His passport had arrived that very day and Roman had packed up his things and left to join the foreign legion.

No, he would not sabotage her dance again.

'I need to go,' Anya said.

'Of course.'

She went into her room and packed her dance bag and pulled on three-quarter tights and a leotard. Over that she put on a tube skirt and a wrapround cardigan.

She arrived at eight, but that was late by her standards. And Mika's.

'Where were you?' he said as barre work commenced. He was working behind her. 'We waited in the foyer for you and then had Reception ring up to your room but there was no answer.'

'I'm not going to be staying at the hotel.'

She could feel his disapproval behind her and the same thing from Lula, who was working in front of her.

Even if Anya wasn't close friends with anyone, they were a close group. They were on tour together and often dined and went out together.

Change was frowned upon.

For Anya the class went beautifully. The whole day did. Her floor work went well, even as she and Mika walked through the second part of *The Firebird*, she was confident, and felt energised, just at the thought that tonight she would see Roman.

'Tonight,' the choreographer said once they were packing up their bags, 'we thought we might go to the open-air cinema at the Vilette Park.'

'I can't make it tonight,' Anya said.

She did not have to give an excuse or a reason, yet as she headed for Roman's she felt as if she should have, for she'd almost heard the silent disapproval from the group as she'd pulled back from them.

Anya tried not to think about it and as she stepped out of the elevator it took a moment to realise that she was alone in his home.

There was no answer when she called out Roman's name. No *Bonjour* returned when she said it out loud.

Anya wandered around.

She looked out at the Seine from the lounge, where the drapes had been drawn last night. Then she walked down the hallway and past grand doors.

One she opened and saw there a huge wooden floored area. Unlike the rest of the house, it was very modern and Anya guessed this would be his gym.

Like Daniil's.

She turned when she heard the elevator and then Roman stepped out.

He was wearing a suit and carrying a laptop bag and it felt like a tiny glimpse of him coming home to her.

'I went to look at an apartment,' he said by way of explaining where he had come from.

'Was it as nice as this?'

'Nowhere is as nice as this,' he said.

He came and joined her and they walked into the room.

'It is like the room at Daniil's,' Anya said. 'You two are so similar, even though you have been apart. Maybe you could put a boxing ring in here…' She guessed at his dream. 'One day you and he can fight again, but fairly this time.'

'Maybe,' Roman said. 'How was class?'

'It was very good.' Anya nodded. 'Well, they are not happy with me, I think, but my dancing went well.'

'Why aren't they happy with you?' He frowned.

'Because I am not staying at the hotel, or joining them tonight.'

'You can go out with them tonight.'

'No.' Anya shook her head. 'Even if you weren't around I wouldn't have gone. It is the open-air cinema and last time I went I got bitten.'

She was so careful with her skin. Roman remembered her telling him to take care where he kissed her because their first time had left her bruised.

'Anyway,' she said, 'I thought we might go out for dinner tonight.'

She wanted to see if things really could be different this time.

Roman nodded.

He needed to know too.

# CHAPTER ELEVEN

SHE WORE A simple black dress and did her make-up carefully.

He looked so elegant in a suit and her stomach was in knots as they were driven through twilit streets but he told the driver they would walk home. He took her to a rooftop restaurant and, as they were led to a sumptuous table that overlooked the Seine, Roman requested somewhere more private instead.

They were seated in a plush velvet booth that muted the sound from fellow diners. He moved the silver candelabrum aside and she liked it that he did. They stared at each other and the candlelight darkened the shadows beneath his cheekbones; she fought with her hand not to reach out to touch his face.

Her heart was fluttering in her chest. She felt that seat belts should be provided, for it was as if she were on a roller-coaster, and she ought to be strapped in.

She felt as if they were on their way to something. Something real, and very beautiful.

And she was scared to hope.

The menu was amazing, but her lazy days spent daydreaming of Roman rather than practising meant that she was careful as she chose.

'The asparagus and orange rind,' she said, and braced herself for him to comment, to point out that it was their first meal out in more than a decade, but he said nothing and simply ordered for himself.

Roman then spoke with the *sommelier* but she shook her head as he translated for her. 'I'll just have water.' Not just that she couldn't afford to indulge, she did not want her guard lowered an inch.

Last night, on seeing his injuries, she had wept so hard and she would not allow herself to do that again.

He did not like the *sommelier's* suggestion to accompany his *côte de veau foyot* and asked for his preferred wine instead. Anya watched as he conversed with ease.

'What are you having to eat?' she asked.

'Veal, with Parmesan and white wine sauce.'

'Your French is excellent,' she commented.

'I know. Even the French think I am French…'

'You are,' Anya responded tartly, alluding to his new identity, but Roman shook his head.

'When people ask where I'm from the answer is, *"Je suis legionnaire."*'

He said it with pride.

'And you also speak English,' Anya commented.

'Not so well. I only started to learn it last year. If I wanted to be able to converse with Daniil and his family…' His voice trailed off.

'So it was no accident you got back in touch.'

She was as observant as he.

Roman thought of the time after Celeste had died, and the mounting need to see for himself how his brother was.

And Anya.

'I didn't know if I would get in touch, but in case I

ever did I wanted to be able to converse…' He gave a slight eye roll.

'Tell me?' Anya said, because, unlike the scars on his back, those tiny facial expressions of his she did still know and could read.

Roman *could* tell her.

For whatever reason, he found that he could talk to her about his twin, when usually he would remain silent.

'When I greeted Libby, I congratulated her on the baby and then Daniil came along and asked where I had been. I told him that I had been in Paris and he was annoyed that I was just an hour away. I asked him, in Russian, how he was. He told me that we were to speak in English in front of his wife.'

He looked into her pale green eyes and they narrowed.

'He's been in England since he was twelve. There was an assumption, given that I had greeted Libby in English, that I was fluent.'

*'Shishka,'* Anya said as she used Daniil's nickname that they had teased him with before he'd gone to be with his new family, and it made Roman smile.

'You should have told him how much effort you went to, just so that you could speak with his family.'

'Perhaps, but I don't want to,' Roman admitted. 'I just don't feel close enough to him to go over things yet.'

'He did try to write to you,' Anya said. 'Libby told me that he did. And he has searched for you, but people who join the French Foreign Legion don't tend to want to be found.'

He stared at the tears that pooled in her eyes and saw the hurt and confusion he had caused.

Only the wine waiter arriving to pour their drinks broke their gaze.

Anya took a sip of her water and breathed.

Then took another sip.

And she was now ready and curious to know.

'What was it like?' she asked, but her voice rose in hurt as she asked the next question. 'When did you apply?' It upset her that he had been filling out application forms while seeing her. That he had been planning to go, even as they'd made love. 'Did you hide the forms from me?'

'There were no forms that I hid,' Roman said. 'You don't apply as such; instead you make your own way there and then you knock on the door,' he explained, and took a sip of his wine.

'And that's it?'

'No.' He shook his head. 'That is just the start of it. All your things are taken from you and you are given a dark uniform and boots and over the next couple of weeks they run many tests on the potential recruits. I was with a real mixed bag of men.' He let out a low laugh as he recalled them. 'A couple didn't even make it through the first day.'

'But you did,' Anya said, happier now that he had not hid applying to join from her. 'What was the training like?'

'Hard,' he admitted. 'You do not get the kepi easily—you have to earn it.'

'Kepi?'

'The white cap we wear,' Roman explained. 'I have never trained harder in my life and then, if you get through that part, you are sent to The Farm and the real hard work begins. There are endless hikes, and physical and psychological obstacles to overcome. Then when I passed, when I got my kepi, I applied for the parachute regiment and went to Corsica.'

'You jumped out of planes?'

'Many times,' he said. 'Then we went on deployments...'

And she asked him something she had been unable to last night and, though she might not like the answer, she was ready to hear it now.

'Did you ever think of me?'

'Not at first.'

He was brutally honest, as was his way, but it did not hurt quite as much as it might have because his admission told her that eventually he had thought of her.

'From the moment you knock at the door, they break you down, they want the strongest of men. You go to The Farm and you train and they break you further. Sometimes you do tasks so mundane that you would go mad if you thought of what you had left behind. Other times you are so exhausted from exertion that there is no time to think. You have to converse in French, and that takes a lot of head space.'

And she listened and imagined him there and was proud that he had done all of those things.

'You wake up and have coffee and bread and jam but you finish that meal and are still hungry. Then there are the endless hikes, and though only you, yourself, have to make it, you start to encourage each other and you start to change, you become a part of a team. We would march, and we would sing songs...'

Anya laughed at that.

'I can't imagine you singing,' she admitted. He was so deep, so private, so undemonstrative, that she could not imagine this man singing with others.

'It is a big part of it,' Roman told her.

And he thought back to that time.

It had been a hike, a long one, and it had been more than testing.

Dario had been falling behind.

*'Suis-moi.'* Roman had told Dario to follow him, to keep up with him, and he had said it in French without thinking.

The night before he had dreamed in French for the first time and he'd felt as if his past was slipping away.

He thought of home rarely; he did not allow himself to. Yet, from a safer distance, he found he could examine his past.

He thought of Daniil and he told himself he was right to have forced him to leave the orphanage. All he could hope was that his twin was doing well.

And he thought of Sev. Yes, a nerd, but he had good brains and Roman hoped that the new school he had attended had helped refine him.

Then he thought of Nikolai and there was a hollow, empty space that ached.

Bleak.

There was bleakness there and then he tried not to think of Anya.

*'Suis-moi,'* he said again to Dario and two of the men ahead started to sing to rally him, and others joined in.

And his past had not slipped away; instead it had drawn in closer and had been right there with him that long-ago day.

He looked at Anya.

'One day, we were hiking and the men started singing. I found myself changing, in my head, the words of a song, to your name...'

'Tell me the song.' Anya asked.

'It is a song of the legion.'

'Tell me the name.'

'"Monica."'

'Tell me the words.'

He would not.

Their meals were served and Anya looked longingly at his dish. The fragrance was amazing and her mouth watered.

'Give me a small piece,' Anya said.

He sliced off a small piece as asked—it was the nicest piece from the middle. He slathered it with the sauce and then held out the fork and she ate from it and closed her eyes in bliss at the taste.

'Is it hard?' Roman asked, because he was curious about her also. 'To deny yourself all the things you love?'

'It is necessary. I want to stay at the top,' she said, 'and that requires discipline.'

'How much longer do you think you will dance for?'

She was suddenly defensive. 'Why do you ask?'

'I'm just curious.'

'I hope that I have another decade in me at the very least.'

She took a drink of water. The conversation was tipping them into the future she knew.

'What if you wanted to have a baby?'

Anya gave him a scornful look.

'Libby retired to have Nadia,' Roman said.

'No, she didn't,' Anya refuted. 'Libby retired because her career was over and *then* she had a baby.' She blew out a breath. 'What is it with men? They expect women to give up their careers and be barefoot and pregnant—'

'Don't be ridiculous, Anya,' he said. 'The last place I want you in is the kitchen. I've had enough of watching you stir stew in your apron to last me a lifetime. And,' he added, 'I've seen your feet. They are not my top fantasy!'

He made her smile, albeit reluctantly.

'Well, I'm not going to retire. Libby might have, and Rachel too, but I shall be dancing well into my forties, I hope. I didn't hit my peak just to give it away.'

And she didn't know how to tell him that she couldn't have babies so she attempted to change the subject. 'How did it go when you caught up with the others?'

Roman, just as he had when Nikolai had swiftly changed the subject, also noticed it when Anya did. He didn't comment, though, he just answered her question.

'Most of it went okay. It was nice to hear what they have been up to. It didn't go well with Daniil, though,' he admitted. 'He has this thought in his head that if he hadn't been adopted we would still have been okay. He is wrong. I lived it, Anya, he did not. Teenage years were hell there and, even if it wasn't to a happy home that he went, at least he got out before that.'

'He doesn't like that you made the decision for him. In the same way I don't like that you chose to end us without discussion.'

'Come on,' Roman said, and called for the bill. 'We are starting to fight and I don't want a fight that doesn't end in bed.'

They chose to walk home, although they went the long way to avoid the square where she had seen him and Celeste kiss.

Back home, he wished her good night.

'I don't want to go to bed.'

'Fine,' Roman said, 'but I do.'

He kissed her in the entrance hall.

A deep kiss, a sensual kiss, but not a teasing one.

He kept his word.

There would be no reward till they could talk properly.

It felt, as she lay in bed alone, unnecessarily cruel.

# CHAPTER TWELVE

'I DIDN'T SLEEP WELL,' Roman said by way of greeting the next morning.

'Nor me.'

He could see the shadows under her eyes and he knew his return had caused them.

There was a selection of herbal teas for her to choose from but Anya chose hot chocolate in the hope it might settle her stomach as she felt a little sick with nerves, wondering how the reception would be when she went to rehearsals.

The berries did not appeal this morning and the thought of yoghurt made her feel queasy.

Roman said nothing as she selected a croissant.

'I'm not looking forward to today,' she admitted.

Yet usually she did.

Usually she woke and rushed to dance.

It troubled her that she had pressed Snooze on her phone and that she felt so tired.

Dance was consuming and so too was Roman. She was honestly scared that there wasn't room for both and that was further put to question when she arrived at the studio.

Until the theatre was available they would rehearse there.

It wasn't ideal and, of course, there was no dressing-room she could hide in.

Instead she had to ride out the uncomfortable vibes. It was a bitchy, vain world at the best of times.

And this wasn't the best of times.

Change was not welcome and Anya removing herself from the hotel was seen as a threat.

She tried to prove it was not, and gave rehearsals her best, but she was tired and a little distracted. By five, when she was ready to go home, Mika insisted they walk through it again.

The choreographer agreed.

When at seven the rest headed out for dinner, Anya and Mika walked through it *again*.

'What the hell is going on, Anya?' the choreographer asked when she forgot one of her routines. 'Stop thinking of going home to your lover and concentrate on your steps.'

She was being punished, Anya knew. She was being tested on where her loyalties lay and they lay with dance when she was here.

Right now, though, she was hungry, but was nervous about saying so. She wanted dinner and a bath and to go to bed.

But she danced instead.

They danced till ten and she made her way home exhausted and very close to tears and she got a little lost. Unwittingly she found herself in the square where she had seen Celeste and Roman kiss.

It remained an agony.

She took the elevator to his apartment and wanted to fall into his arms but there was no Roman waiting.

No response when she called out.

She pushed his bedroom door open and, no, he was not there.

He was never there when she really needed him.

And then she wandered some more and pushed open a room, more beautiful than any she had ever seen.

It was a nursery.

Lemon wallpaper dressed the walls and the silk drapes were cream. A silver antique cot was in the centre and it hurt too much to go in so she hastily closed the door.

The next room was an equal torture.

Pretty in pink, the child's bed was dressed in satin and roses, and Anya was in tears as she stepped out.

She could hear the elevator and tried to stop crying but she couldn't

'Anya?' Roman said, and went to take her in his arms, but she pushed him back.

'Where have you been?'

'Josie's granddaughter is sick. My driver is on vacation, as is half of Paris at this time, so I drove them to the airport myself.' He had never had to offer such explanations, but he did. 'That's not why you're crying, though.'

It wasn't.

It was the wretched couple of days at work; it was the memory of Roman and Celeste and, worse, just so raw right now, the babies that could never fill these rooms.

She didn't know how to tell him.

She simply couldn't bring herself to.

Her eating, or rather lack of it, had been such an issue with them all those years ago.

She thought of their row on the night he had caught her vomiting.

It was by her own doing that she hadn't had periods.

There hadn't been one for more than a year.

'Come here,' he said, and took her in his arms. 'We can talk about it. Whatever it is, surely we can talk?'

'We can't,' she sobbed, and she kissed him instead.

She wanted the oblivion that she found his bed.

And Roman could fight it no more and wanted the same thing.

But even the silken kiss he delivered could not banish the memory of what she had seen that terrible day in the square.

Oh, she tried.

She kissed him back hard but it would not erase that image. There were tears streaming down her cheeks, wetting their kiss, and he tasted them, yet still it could not erase the pain.

Her body was a heated mix of desire and rage and confusion and Anya pulled back.

'You're not helping. I need to go back to the hotel.'

'You don't.'

'I do. I'm behind with my dance. I need to give it my full focus and I just can't when I'm with you.'

'Anya—' he started, and she could not bear the voice of reason when her emotions were all over the place so she stopped him.

'If you really care for me, you will let me leave,' Anya said. 'We don't work together, Roman. I can't focus on my craft when I am with you. Surely we should know that by now.'

He packed her things but as his car pulled up at the hotel he caught her hand as she went to get out.

'You're wrong,' he said.
'I'm not,' Anya said. 'Don't call me.'
'I shan't.'
'Don't come here.'
'I won't.'
She felt as if the safety ropes had been cut.
Roman always meant what he said.

# CHAPTER THIRTEEN

SHE WAS FORGIVEN for her brief absence when they all met in the foyer the following morning and her colleagues greeted her warmly when they found out she had moved back to the hotel.

Anya, though, could not forgive them.

Always she gave her dance her all, and she was angry at her troupe for their doubt in her, and it showed in each rehearsal.

Nothing was working.

Her body, usually fluid and flexible, felt brittle and like hardening wax.

'It will come together when we get to the theatre,' the choreographer reassured her.

And Anya held onto that as she suffered through frustrating days when her body refused to yield, and she ached through lonely nights.

She always gave her dance everything, yet she felt now as if she had nothing to give.

Always she had danced for Roman.

For the solider she grieved for or to the memory of them.

Now it felt as if she had removed herself from her source.

How she wept for him and loathed that he had let her go back to the hotel without a fight.

He had.

Unlike Anya, Roman was patient.

He set about the renovations.

His dream was not a gym in memory of his brother. Instead mirrors were put in and a barre ran the length of the wall. The floors were polished.

He avoided walking near the hotel or the theatre as he did not want to upset her.

He knew, though, when the dance company had moved there, because there was a small piece on the news.

Mika and Anya were being interviewed and, of course, he watched.

'Are you excited to be back in Paris?'

'I am thrilled,' Anya answered through a translator. 'I have such fond memories of the last time I was here.'

And she smiled, and so too did Roman, for he could taste the vinegar in her smile from here and knew that it was aimed at him.

'How are rehearsals going?'

It was Mika who answered, again through a translator. 'We have a full dress rehearsal tomorrow.'

'The chemistry when you two perform—' the interviewer started, but Roman flicked off the television.

He did not want to know.

And yet they had to face these things so he turned the television back on and got the end of Mika's response to the question.

'To dance,' Mika said, 'is to love. Without love you cannot dance.'

Mika was right, it would seem, for without love Anya could not dance.

She hated that she could not speak of Celeste and she loathed her own jealousy.

She felt flushed in the face with the hurt of it all and cross, most of all, with herself.

She loved him so much.

She was teary and fragile as they prepared for full dress rehearsal on the day before opening night. Anya raised her arm as her costume was done up and she remembered Roman carefully pulling the zip down.

It would not do up by a fraction.

But that fraction had the costume manager tutting. Really she had only put on a couple of pounds but it meant that her costume would have to be let out.

She was scolded for the weight gain. She sat in the dressing-room on the edge of tears and took out her phone and again resisted calling him.

Instead she looked up a song.

A song from the French foreign legion named 'Monica', or 'La Monique', and as it played she read the translation.

The lyrics were so beautiful that tears spilled from her eyes as she found out that Roman had thought of her all along.

She needed him, more than she ever had, and the temptation was too much. With the phone in her hand and those words on the screen, she called him. As he answered, just hearing his voice pulled her back to the vortex of them and Anya let out a sob, hung up and turned off her phone.

She needed to focus for her performance tomorrow and whenever they were together they argued.

The costume manager came in with the spare costume as it was a little larger to allow for seams being taken in or let out. It didn't add to her confidence as she dressed.

She stood at the edge of the stage and waited to go on, but this afternoon she felt wooden.

For this rehearsal they would not dance properly. It was too exhausting and that energy would be saved for the audience. They would walk through all the steps and do some jetés, though not at peak, and Mika would perform some lifts on her.

The whole rehearsal from start to finish went terribly.

It was the worst final rehearsal that Anya had ever had. She did not feel light in Mika's arms and it would seem the trust in each other was gone.

Once she leapt and Mika mistimed things but as he caught her he could not correct and, embarrassed by his own clumsy performance, he put her down.

'Christmas must be coming early,' Mika said nastily, and she could hear a few sniggers as he continued. 'Because Firebird is getting fat.'

The rest of the rehearsal was just as hellish, and when it ended, the choreographer did not offer the platitude of it all coming together for opening night.

Instead she was in a huddle with the director and Anya felt sick, for she knew she wasn't the only one with doubts about her suitability for tomorrow night.

She could feel the panic starting to build. Tomorrow was opening night and not one single rehearsal had gone well.

She went to try on her altered costume before heading back to the hotel, but as she stepped in she saw Lula, her understudy, trying the firebird costume on.

She was, Anya was sure, about to be cut.

She fled to her dressing-room and usually she would shower and change but instead she just wiped off her make-up and dressed.

And then, as she left, she picked up all her useless, stupid trinkets and stuffed them into her bag.

They weren't working.

Nothing worked without Roman.

She didn't know what to do. She held it in and left without saying goodbye as she often did, but as Anya pushed open the exit door she could hold it in no more and she started to sob.

But there, waiting for her, was Roman and she fell into his arms and wept into his chest as he told her that it would all be okay.

Roman, having answered her call and heard her small sob, had rung straight back but Anya, being Anya, had turned off her phone.

He did not want to disrupt the rehearsal and so he had waited outside.

'I'm going to lose the part…'

'You're not.'

'I am.'

'Anya, you're not.'

'You don't know that. I can't dance, I've been rehearsing over and over and I can't do it and I've just seen Lula, my understudy, trying on Firebird—'

'Today was dress rehearsal?' Roman checked, and Anya nodded into his chest. 'Doesn't everyone try on their costumes today?'

'Yes, but Mika and I are fighting. He said…' She closed her eyes. She was too humiliated to repeat what Mika had said.

Roman closed his eyes too. Of course she and Mika were fighting. He could hardly stand to hear about their rows, or Mika's reaction to Roman's arrival.

He would listen, though, if it made things easier for her.

'What did he say?' Roman asked.

'I don't want to tell you.'

'Come home,' he offered.

'No, I'm going to go to the dance studio and go through it alone.'

'How many times have you done that?'

So many times, Anya thought.

'Whatever you're doing isn't working,' Roman pointed out.

'No.'

'So why not try something different?'

They walked and they could go the long way and avoid the square where she had seen them kiss, but she had avoided so much and it was getting them nowhere so they walked through it.

And his arm was around hers and it hurt less and less.

'I've made you a light supper—' he started, and Anya turned in surprise.

'You cook?'

'Yes,' Roman said. 'Josie and her husband are coming back tonight. I've sent my driver to pick them up this time. You can have a nice bath and then something to eat, then sleep.'

He calmed her—he always had.

Oh, he enthralled her and made her burn but he was so strong and so measured that with him she felt safe with her wild emotions.

They arrived back at the apartment and again Anya felt soothed as she stood in the entrance hall.

It felt good to be home.

'Why don't you go and have a bath?' Roman suggested.

'Do I smell?' Anya asked.

'Just a bit.' He smiled and he made *her* smile.

She ran the deepest bath and peeled off her clothes and the scented, oily water was relaxing to her aching limbs so she lay there for a generous while.

And then she felt the pull of her body to be with him. She put on her robe and walked through to the kitchen.

His back was to her and he was wearing black jeans and no top and his scars were becoming familiar to her now.

She went up behind him and kissed his shoulder and then looked at what he was making.

He was turning out a crab tartare, one of several, and she dipped her finger in a dish filled with red and tasted that it was *hren*, a horseradish relish, and one of her favourite foods from home.

It was what she had ordered at the restaurant that terrible time.

Yet now he had made it.

'I love *hren*,' she said.

'I remember.'

She watched as he sautéed wild chanterelles, and the scent of the mushrooms made her stomach growl.

It really was the perfect supper for the night before such a performance and, had she eaten out tonight, this was what she might well have chosen.

And it was also the perfect company to be in when your nerves were in shreds.

Some considered Roman to be lacking in emotion.

Anya had always known different.

The emotions were there, and she felt them. His calm presence tonight was for her.

'Did you learn to cook in the legion?' she asked him.

'The only thing I learnt about cooking there was to open cans.'

'Was the food awful?'

'It did its job.'

'So, when did you learn to cook like this?'

'Anya,' Roman said 'let's not do this tonight.'

'Celeste?' Anya asked, and said her name without venom.

Roman nodded. 'Let's go through.'

There were so many parts of his life still missing. Her dancing had suffered since his return, not because of Roman, she was starting to realise, but because of her own dark thoughts and fears.

They ate at the table, and it had been beautifully laid, with silver and candles, which Roman lit.

And Celeste must have taught him this also, Anya thought, for there was no silver service at the orphanage, she knew for sure, and she guessed it was the same at the foreign legion.

There was a burn of jealousy, but she breathed through it.

Roman drank wine, Anya water, and she looked over as he loaded his plate.

And she tasted the crab, so fresh that she knew it must have been prepared from scratch after she had called him.

And all this would not be possible without Celeste, Anya knew.

They would not be sitting having such a romantic meal, Roman, his top half naked, she in a robe, and eating this sumptuous dinner that he had prepared for her, without the years they could not speak of.

Celeste was a part of his complex journey and not

knowing a part of his life felt worse than the jealousy that choked her.

'Tell me about her,' Anya said.

'No,' Roman said. 'Tonight you need calm.'

'I'm ready to hear. I need to know, Roman, I know I get jealous…'

'I don't want to hurt you Anya,' he said. 'And I don't want you speaking badly of her.'

'I will try not to.'

Roman nodded. He did not want to upset her further tonight, but maybe the decks needed to be cleared.

'What do you want to know?'

'All of it,' she said. 'I want to know why you were looking for a wife.'

'Just as I was about to leave, some friends showed me an advert. It was a joke at first…'

'What did the advert say?'

'Just that she wanted company—someone to go to the theatre with and things like that.'

'And to share her bed?'

'Yes.'

'I want to know what the advert said.'

'She said that her father was dying and he had wanted to see her married. Celeste had given up on love but she wanted to make her father happy. She hoped the marriage would last for two years. She spoke of the ballet and theatre, and that she liked to cook but preferred to eat out.'

'Roman?' Anya pushed.

'She wanted someone good looking, preferably younger than her…'

'Roman?' Anya pushed again. 'Did the advert imply sex?'

He told her but he was not cruel.

She had a performance tomorrow and to mention *adventurous* would provoke the screams of Firebird being plucked alive.

'She said that as well as all that, she wanted a sexual partner.'

'So you were just a sex toy.'

'Yes,' Roman said, and he could leave it there but it would be a lie and a cop-out and Celeste deserved better than that. So too did Anya. They needed the truth if they were to survive so he amended, 'At first.'

His words cut like a knife, because him as a sex toy she could almost, *almost*, deal with, but never his affection for another woman, never that it might have turned to love.

'Do you want to hear this?' he checked. 'Are you sure you need to hear this tonight?'

Anya nodded and then shook her head. 'You could have come to Saint Petersburg and been with me,' she said. 'You say you were rich by then, whereas I was barely making ends meet...'

'Anya, if you want to hear this then you need to listen properly. I never intended to come and find you.'

'But why not?'

'Pride,' he said.

'Foolish pride.'

'No.' He shook his head. 'I would do it all again because the man I was would not have sat back and let you do what you had to to get by in the dance world. Celeste taught me patience.'

'No, that was me,' Anya said, and she remembered the burn of their first time, how he would have had her in a moment and that she had slowed him down.

'She taught me manners,' Roman said.

'No,' Anya refuted. 'That was also me.'

'I'm not talking about please and thank you in the bedroom…' Roman countered.

Anya was.

'And what else did Saint Celeste teach you?' she asked with a sneer, but her face soon crumpled and she knew he would terminate the conversation. 'I am trying…' she pleaded.

'I know,' he said, and instead of telling her off he took her hand.

Roman had known this would be a difficult conversation, which was why he hadn't wanted to go there tonight. His reaction would be just the same if Anya spoke of Mika or another lover she'd had.

Soon it would be his turn, to sit lacerated as she told him about Mika, and so for now he kept it at Celeste.

'She taught me how to hold a fine china cup and how to sit in a restaurant…'

And she winced because their last night had been spent in a restaurant.

'Remember how I embarrassed you.'

'You did not.'

'But I did,' Roman said. 'Decorum was part of your curriculum…'

'I could have shown you,' she pleaded.

'But I didn't want you teaching me.'

'You let her, though!'

'Because I did not care for her then. Celeste and I had a deal, two years together, and I intended to use them wisely.'

'So you answered the ad…'

'Yes.'

'And you made love to her.'

'Sex,' Roman said.

'With affection?' she asked, and then changed her mind. 'I don't want to know.'

'You do need to hear this, Anya,'

Roman had decided.

It was time.

'I was locked in the secure unit for four years. I had no social skills, it is not a part of the orphanage's curriculum.'

His words were cutting and she nodded her understanding that it still hurt him to recall those times and Roman continued.

'I remember when I went first to her home. I had never been inside one, not a proper home.'

And she thought how bleak his life had been at the bedsit that he had tried to make presentable for her.

'Was that the first time you saw her?'

'Yes, we had exchanged photos and spoken on the phone, but that was our first meeting. Celeste too was shocked,' Roman recalled. 'She said, "You look like your picture..."'

And Anya smiled for the first time about the subject.

'Did you sleep with her that day?'

'No,' Roman said, and he held her angry glare. 'That night.'

'And?'

'I would never discuss what went on in the bedroom with you and I shall extend the same courtesy to Celeste. All I shall say is that affection grew. Anya, when I turned up at Daniil's Libby embraced me. When I turned up at Celeste's door and she did the same I recoiled.'

Anya could not speak.

'I wanted to improve myself. Which I did. If you don't approve of my methods, that is up to you.'

'I don't approve...' she said, and then she closed her eyes. 'I don't know.' She looked at him. 'It was supposed to last only two years, yet it went on for longer?'

'Celeste found out that she was dying. I chose to be with her till the end.'

And how could she hate him for that?

'What is your new name?' she asked.

It was the only question he wasn't prepared for.

'Roman?' Anya begged. 'Surely you can tell me that.'

It was so hard to, though. 'I wanted to give my brother a chance of a life without his poor relation on his back. I wanted you to have the life you deserved. I couldn't turn my back on it all, though.'

'I don't understand.'

'I was given a new identity—we all are for that first year. Then you get a choice, retain the new one or go back to the old. If I kept my new one, I could never look you up, I could never see my brother again. And I couldn't do it. I am still Roman Zverev.'

'So why have you stayed away all these years?' she asked.

'Because I never felt ready, because I still thought I would be a strain...'

'So, what, you had to change before you could find me?'

'I didn't do for you, Anya, I did it for me.'

Anya sat there as he stood.

'I am not going to apologise for Celeste. Get used to that,' he said. 'Anya, had we stayed together we would have been as poor as church mice and I tell you now...' he made a gesture with two fingers to the back of his throat, and her own throat closed as he touched on a painful subject '…I could not have put up with that. I *would* have held you back.'

He was done explaining, and left the table and went through to the bedroom.

He lay on his back with his hands behind his head. He loathed sharing his feelings, he loathed to admit that need for Anya that had clawed at his heart.

And Anya came to the door and she remembered a time many, many years ago.

Flu had swept through the orphanage. In an effort to contain it, all the orphans had been confined to their dormitories and rooms.

Katya too had been ill and Anya had been asked to work in the kitchen. She had taken suppers around on a trolley without the perpetual guard of her mother.

As she'd looked in she had seen Roman, lying on his bed, his hands behind his head.

He hadn't been sick but had been confined.

The guard had opened the door and she had gone in.

Roman had stared up at the ceiling and had not turned to look, for he'd expected it to be Katya bringing him his meal.

'One day you will get out of here and do great things,' Anya had said, and his face had turned towards her.

Anya smiled at the recollection.

He was out of there and had done great things.

He'd done them in his own unique way, and she was proud that he had.

'How did you get the chocolate?' she had asked as she had walked towards him, carrying his tray.

He hadn't answered.

Instead he had smiled.

She had walked into his room utterly innocent, but he had stripped her bare with his eyes. She had walked over, her eyes on his crotch, watching him harden.

His eyes had been on her breasts, which had ached.

'What time are lights out?' she had asked.

'Ten.'

'Anya.' A worker had called for her to hurry, but their love had been born by then.

And at ten that night she had lain in her own bed and thought of him, and Roman had done the same as her.

'You did get out of there, Roman,' Anya said, and he turned and looked. 'And you have done great things.'

'I had to do it by myself, for myself.'

Anya nodded, even if she did not quite understand.

Now, though, she could do as she had wanted to back then. She walked towards him, and he smiled as she stripped herself of her robe.

# CHAPTER FOURTEEN

'YOU'RE NOT SUPPOSED to be here,' Roman warned as she walked towards him. 'No sex before a match…'

'Sergio had no idea,' Anya said. 'Anyway, I'm not a boxer.'

She bent her head and kissed his sulky mouth as she had wanted to back then.

And he stroked her breasts.

His kiss felt like a delicious reward, and all the promise of his mouth and the skill of his tongue and cares and worries faded.

She stroked him, unzipped him and he kicked his jeans off. Their mouths barely parted.

As she knelt over him his mouth took her breast and sent little volts of pleasure through her body. Her breast felt hot, tender, and he roused in her an endless ache.

'No bruises,' she warned.

He knew now.

'Turn over,' she said, and though her voice was husky with lust there was something she had to do.

And she did.

She looked at his back and now he liked the soft kisses she rained there. He thought of that time and the sand, like salt in wounds, and now they were bathed by the salt of her tears. He thought of that long, lonely night she had been by his side, even if not physically.

He liked too the heat of her sex in the small of his back yet he rolled them over because he wanted more.

There was no better feeling than being taken by Roman and she could feel the warmth spread through her, a deep, enduring warmth that was always waiting for him.

She looked at him and the surroundings did not matter when she was with him.

They could have been anywhere—teenagers in a shabby room with a silver-grey sky streaming through a small window, or in this luxurious apartment—but the feelings were, and had always been, the same.

She centred on him, and when he moved it was slowly and with a precision only Roman could achieve.

He knew her needs, and her need was him.

She moved her hands over his back to feel the skin and the muscles that were taut beneath her fingers.

When her head arched he kissed her neck and found a spot so tender that her hips rose.

And he simply knew.

There was the sound of them and the feeling of him and it was a place where Anya could voice doubt.

'If you leave me again, never come back.'

'I'm never leaving you.'

And then his pace quickened, and that powerful body at full thrust was dizzying.

His buttocks were firm and she dug her fingers in and held on, not to him but to herself because her thighs were shaking and there was a rush of heat.

Every part of her was taut and on the edge and then he stilled, and she watched his jaw grit and then as he came

she toppled beneath him. An orgasm so intense that there
was no breath in her body. The power that shot into her
seemed to stun her and then the weight of him for a moment, as their bodies pulsed as one.

'Why do you say I'll leave you?'

'Because you did.'

Because you still might.

Still he had not told her he loved her.

The jigsaw of them was complete, the jigsaw of Roman
was she thought, too.

She wanted to tell him that there could never be babies but she did not want to spoil the night and she looked
at him.

'There's something I have to tell you, and I am scared
you will be cross.'

'Don't be scared.' He guessed that she was talking
about Mika.

'I don't want to tell you tonight. I'm tired, and I'm
worried about tomorrow.'

'Then sleep,' he said. 'It will keep.'

And she lay in his arms and told him a truth.

'Life's harder without you in it, Roman.'

He didn't believe it, she knew.

'You need to tell Daniil what you told me.'

'I shall.'

'Now.'

'It's midnight.'

'Do you think he would care about that?'

'No.'

'Then call him.'

Roman did.

His voice was soothing and sad too, and she lay listening to this proud man explain to his twin all he just had told her.

And she fell asleep thinking of *Firebird* and hoping that tomorrow she could dance for him.

# CHAPTER FIFTEEN

'*Bonjour, mademoiselle.*'

Josie was back in the kitchen as Anya passed by, but this time from the direction of Roman's room.

It had been bliss to wake in his bed, even if Roman hadn't been in it.

'*Bonjour*, Josie,' Anya called, and then remembered that Josie's granddaughter had been sick and, in terrible French, enquired about her.

She was doing much better, as far as Anya could make out.

'*Bon!*' Anya smiled.

She headed to the balcony and Roman put his paper down. Neither had to enquire how the other had slept.

It had been bliss.

She poured a hot chocolate and ate some berries.

'The cast list goes up at ten,' Anya said.

'You'll be on it.'

'I'm not so sure.'

The nerves were starting to come back, though that was to be expected given that tonight was opening night.

'Do you want——?' Roman started, but his question was interrupted by a loud scream from Josie and he jumped up and moved quickly to see what the problem was.

And then Anya saw Roman smile as a hysterical Josie spoke to him excitedly.

He turned and explained the problem to a bemused Anya. 'Josie had seen me on the balcony and then opened the elevator...'

Daniil was walking in, with Libby beside him, holding little Nadia and laughing.

'Roman mustn't have mentioned that he had an identical twin,' Libby said. 'The doorman opened the elevator and we came straight up.'

'I had the same thing happen at your place,' Roman said, but Libby's eyes had drifted to Anya, who sat in her robe and had obviously come from Roman's bed.

'Caught!' Anya said.

'We'd already guessed!' Libby grinned. 'Anya, we just had to come and see Roman after he called last night, and—I'm going to be terribly rude—is there any chance...?'

'You want tickets for tonight?' Anya smiled. 'Of course. Sev and Naomi are flying in too and I have left tickets for Rachel at the box office. We should call Nikolai...'

'He'll be on his yacht in the middle of nowhere,' Daniil said.

Roman wasn't so sure. He looked at his brother, who had come all these miles just to speak with him face to face.

'I understand now,' Daniil said, and they embraced. 'I'm sorry,' Daniil admitted, ashamed at insisting that Roman speak in English.

'No need,' Roman said.

Anya didn't want to go to work.

It was so wonderful to catch up, she wanted to sit and

laugh and reminisce, but she really could not be late this morning.

'Get ready,' Roman said when he saw the time.

She went back to her pretty bedroom and put on her dance clothes and then a taupe linen wrap dress and flat shoes. She checked her bag and then went back out onto the balcony to say goodbye.

Libby smiled when she saw her. 'Are you off?'

'I have to rehearse and then check the cast list…' She closed her eyes as she recalled how terrified she'd been yesterday.

How terrified she was now.

It seemed such a long time ago but now nerves were starting to flood back and they were fierce because she had friends coming to see her and it would be the ultimate let down and embarrassment if she was cut.

'There's a chance it won't be me that you see perform as Firebird tonight,' she admitted, and her cheeks went red as she did.

She glanced over at Roman but he just rolled his eyes as if she was mad to even think she was about to be cut.

Anya explained further to Libby. 'I've had a difficult time at rehearsals and yesterday was terrible.' Her jaw gritted as Roman gave an exaggerated yawn.

'Well, if you want to catch up once the cast list is up, just say,' Libby offered, because, though she hadn't reached Anya's heights, she knew all about being cut and knew that Anya might want to regroup well away from the theatre and even away from Roman and Daniil.

'It might give these two a chance to catch up.'

Anya hesitated. She liked to be alone on the day of a performance but she recalled Roman's words, that whatever she had been doing these past couple of weeks hadn't been working.

Usually she would go back to her hotel room and take a nap, or rather pretend to relax and mentally prepare for tonight's performance.

Maybe it was time to try something different.

'Whatever happens, I finish at one,' Anya said. 'Perhaps we could meet and…' She gave a small tense shrug. 'I can't do a big lunch on the day of a performance.'

'Of course not,' Libby said. 'How about we look at the shops?'

It sounded like something to look forward to and Anya nodded.

She went to head out and there was Josie, still flustered at having Daniil arrive, and she was coming out of the gym with a broom.

The door didn't close behind her and Anya glanced in.

It wasn't a gym.

And even if he had never told her, Anya knew then that she was loved.

In her time away, mirrors had been put in and there was a barre where she could rehearse.

She wanted to go and thank him, but this morning was for Roman and his twin so she headed for the theatre.

Anya walked quickly and as she went through the square she forgot that this was where she had seen him kiss Celeste as the nerves danced and fluttered in her throat and chest.

She took her place at the barre and the morning was long.

For everyone.

All anyone wanted was the cast list to be put up.

And finally it was.

She tried to walk slowly and not show her fear.

'Firebird, Tatania.'

Even seeing it written, she still could not quite believe she had made it. A part of her had thought, after two weeks of terrible rehearsals, that she might be dropped.

Mika was there, relieved to see that he was still Ivan the Prince after yesterday's rehearsal disaster.

It really was a cutthroat world and things changed in an instant.

Perhaps that was why she loved it so much, Anya thought.

She watched as Mika walked off and if they were to dance well tonight then there was something that needed to be said.

'Hey.' She knocked on his dressing-room door and he called for her to enter.

'Mika, I need you to make me look good, just as much as you need me. Don't you ever speak like that to me again.'

She didn't wait for his response; instead she went to try on her costume.

Her costume had been let out but as she tried it on she felt it pull at the bust, and the costume manager said nothing but her jaw gritted as she would be spending the afternoon letting it out a couple of millimetres more.

Anya left the theatre for a few precious hours. It was a hive of activity—costumes were being steamed and delivered to dressing-rooms, wigs were being prepared and, though she would usually go back to the hotel and rest, she smiled as she headed off to meet Libby.

'Well!' Libby said when she saw Anya's smile. 'I don't need to ask!'

'I am very relieved,' Anya admitted. 'I really wasn't sure if I would be Firebird tonight. Things are tense back there and the costume manager is not speaking to me.' Anya rolled her eyes. 'I've put on a little weight.'

'Well, you look amazing for it,' Libby said. 'I need to find a dress to wear tonight.'

And there was no place nicer to shop than Paris. Libby found something for the performance in a very dark shade of crimson that looked fabulous with her blond hair and Anya held Nadia while Libby went to try it on.

She wanted a baby.

Never had she fully admitted it to herself, but holding Nadia, so precious and tiny, Anya felt tears sting at the back of her eyes.

She stood up, refusing to give in to them. She knew that she would look mad sitting in the middle of a luxury boutique crying her eyes out.

Instead she examined the clothes and held up a dress that was nothing like she would ever choose normally. It was a halter-neck and the colours of a peacock's tail in full display, and beside it were shoes that were a little high for Anya, but not too high.

'What do you think?' Libby asked as she came out of the dressing-room.

'You look wonderful,' Anya told her. 'You certainly don't look as if you've just had a baby.'

'Well, ballet has helped with that…' Libby started, but then changed topic in mid-sentence when she saw the dress that Anya was holding. 'Anya, you have to try that on.'

'I don't like halter-necks…' Anya said, but then she decided that she might as well see what it looked like on.

And with the shoes too.

She examined herself in the mirrors. The dress showed her back and every last inch of her slender arms but she liked it and she remembered Roman had told her to stop covering herself up.

And why did she?

Yes, she was very slim but she looked after her body and was proud of it.

'Oh, Anya!' Libby's jaw dropped when Anya stepped out. 'I've never seen you in anything other than grey or beige—you look amazing.'

'Taupe,' Anya corrected. 'I don't wear beige.'

But she did love the dress.

So much so that she decided to wear it home. It was summery outside and she felt summery on the inside today now that she was free from her anger about Celeste.

She wasn't angry any more. If anything, she thought of Roman's wife fondly, because Roman had never known a home till then.

As she and Libby walked through the square where Anya had seen Roman and Celeste kissing, she thought about a woman who'd had the courage to ask for what she'd wanted.

And the universe had sent her Roman!

Anya shocked Libby by suddenly laughing out loud.

'I was just thinking of…' she smiled as she said it now '…Roman and his wife.'

'So,' Libby asked, because she simply couldn't resist, 'how long have you and Roman been seeing each other?'

'A few weeks…' Anya said, and then Libby nudged her and Anya laughed again and told the truth.

'He had my heart a very long time ago.'

There were two surprises waiting for them when they got back.

Sev and Naomi were out on the balcony and Rachel had arrived.

'Rachel!' Anya kissed her on the cheeks. 'I was hoping to see you. I left your tickets at the box office—' And then she broke off when she saw that Rachel was wearing a wedding ring.

Three surprises.

'What's this?' Anya asked, and then frowned as yet another surprise arrived and she saw that Nikolai was here.

And wearing a wedding ring too.

'You two!' Anya said. 'But I didn't even know you were seeing each other.'

'Well, you can talk,' Rachel said.

'But when did this happen?'

'A couple of weeks ago.' Rachel gleefully showed off her ring. 'We're going to be living in Belgravia and…' she turned and smiled at Sev and Naomi '…we're coming to see you in New York at the new year.'

'I knew,' Roman said.

'How?' Rachel frowned.

'Nikolai did not want to speak of who he was dating and I saw Rachel sitting, waiting, on the dock when we got off his yacht.'

'And you didn't tell me?' Anya said.

'I don't tell you everything, Anya.' And he watched as her eyes narrowed at the tease—there were things she didn't yet know.

It was a wonderful catch up of friends.

Yes, friends.

As they chatted about Nikolai and Rachel's secret wedding, Anya watched Libby pass little Nadia to Daniil, who held his daughter both easily and tenderly.

She wanted this for Roman.

And it hurt to know that it was something she could not give him.

'I have to go,' she said at four.

It had been a lovely day but she needed to get into the right head space to perform as the firebird tonight.

'*Merde,*' Libby said.

'Doesn't *merde* mean shit in French?' Sev asked.

Anya laughed. 'It is a superstition that it would be bad luck to wish a dancer good luck before a performance.'

And then the nicest thing happened.

'Oh,' Rachel said, 'before you go, Anya, I've got something for you.'

Anya took the present and opened it with a frown and then smiled as she took out a slender glass case. Inside it was a white feather.

'It's from both my wedding dress *and* my favourite costume…'

'Which she stole,' Libby said.

Anya opened the clasp and took out the feather.

'It reminds me of you when you dance…' Rachel said.

'Thank you so much,' Anya said. It really was a thoughtful gift. 'I shall have it in my dressing-room.'

'Here,' Libby said, and there was another present, a little porcelain thing with long dangly legs that Anya recognised from the gym at Daniil's. And, though she was sure it wasn't the same one, she knew that this gift was something precious to Libby and Daniil and that too would sit on her dressing table.

Naomi stood then. 'I had no idea how superstitious you lot were about opening night but we brought you these…'

It was a massive bag of peanut-butter cups and perhaps the sweetest of gifts. They had seen her sneaking food and had simply accepted her.

Anya hugged her.

Naomi didn't know the dance world and gave a blink of surprise at the delight with which Anya received the gift.

'I will keep the foil from tonight forever.'

'Oh, she will,' Roman said, and then he looked at Anya. 'Do you want me to walk you to the theatre?'

'Thank you.'

They didn't speak much as they walked and Anya apologised for that. 'I need to focus now on tonight.''

'Whatever suits you,' he said. 'And that dress does.'

Anya smiled. 'It was nice, shopping with Libby.'

They walked through warm Paris streets and through the square and, yes, she had forgiven him for marrying Celeste.

Roman was right. She could not have had this career and their intensity back then. It had been too consuming and also Roman was right that they would have been as poor as mice and he would never have accepted being kept by her.

But there was another reason she was quiet.

Anya knew she could not dance well tonight with the weight of what she knew she had to reveal.

They were at the stage door and she remembered their first kiss long ago by a stage door back home and so did he.

'You were right,' she said.

'I know,' he replied, and then smiled. 'About what?'

'Roman, I am not a prodigy. I have seen dancers younger than me rise faster. I had to work and be selfish and absorbed to get here. I didn't fail that audition because of you. I have not been chosen for many parts since that day. Two years ago, when I made Lilac Fairy, it was by chance. Some of the critics said I was a rather large Lilac Fairy and so I regrouped. When I understudied as Firebird, I was more selfish than ever. I trained harder, I put all I had into sculpting my body for the part in case the time came when I could perform it. When Daniil and Libby saw me that first night as Firebird, it was no accident that I performed well. I had waited for my moment and planned for it, but there were consequences to that choice.'

The perfectionist must now tell the person who mattered the most to her that, no, she was not perfect.

And it had to be now because she could not dance with the weight of it, not even for one more night.

'I can't have children, Roman.'

He looked deep into her eyes.

'Because of my eating I have stopped menstruating. It is my own fault. I'm so sorry.'

'Why are you saying sorry to me?'

'Because I believe that you love me.'

Still he did not answer.

'And,' Anya said, 'if you do then it affects you.'

'Anya—'

'No,' she interrupted him. 'I don't want your knee-jerk reaction. I don't want you to tell me it does not matter when we both know that it does. I know that one day you will resent me for it.'

'No.'

'Oh, but you shall. When I don't eat or I practise too hard, you will remind me of the cost of that choice. I cannot bear the thought of you blaming me.'

'Never.'

'Please, don't.' She put up her hand to his face and she remembered the first time she'd done that and he had flinched but he did not now. Theirs was a very precious love and she would tell the truth. 'You do care and so do I. You said yourself that Daniil has everything you ever wanted.'

'I wasn't talking about Nadia,' Roman said. 'I meant that he was happy that he had a family he adored. He still would have, even if it was just him and Libby. Anya, I admire how you have pushed yourself, how you have given up so much for nights like tonight. And I respect it too. It's up to you whether or not you believe me.'

And she told him another truth. 'Every time I dance, I dance for you.'

But then Roman, the man who had always had her heart, told her again that it was time for something to be different.

'Anya, tonight go out there and dance for yourself.'

'For me?'

'Yes, for you. You have worked for this, you deserve the reward.'

He gave her a kiss, a long slow one that really ought to lead to the bedroom, but he let her go and then at the sound of footsteps Anya watched as his jaw tightened.

*'Privyet.'* Mika said hi as he walked past them.

It was time to go in.

'I'll be watching,' Roman said.

It was nice to know.

Only as she headed in through the stage door did Anya realise she hadn't told Roman that she and Mika weren't and never had been an item.

Oh, poor Roman, having to watch them perform tonight, Anya thought, and then, for the second time that day, found herself laughing out loud.

'Anya!'

There were calls of greeting and also a sense of relief because Anya had arrived, and she was usually here by now.

She waved back and went into her dressing-room, breathed and centred herself, had a shower and preparations began.

She took out her feather and the little pink thing with dangly legs and placed them on her dressing table.

And she took out a peanut-butter cup, which would be her treat and energy booster during the interval.

Her peacock-swirl dress had been hung up and she would wear it later tonight, Anya decided.

Then she thought of Roman and was starting to believe not just in his love but that they could make it.

She took out the little trinkets that told of their love and she knew more about him now.

The earrings were now a pair.

Every time she had danced it had been for him.

But Roman was right. Tonight she would dance for herself.

Her friends, good friends, were in the audience to support her and so too was the love of her life.

And he knew the truth now.

Now she could dance for herself, and claim for herself the reward for the hard work it had taken to get to this point.

She applied the finishing touches to her make up and secured her headpiece.

The costume manager came in for one final check.

Anya looked at her reflection.

She was shaking with nerves as she made her way through the maze of corridors to the stage. She stood there, battling nausea, but today it would not abate and she called for a bucket.

No one was surprised. This was backstage after all and nerves were the motivator.

'Better?' Mika checked, after Anya had rinsed her mouth and the make-up lady had come and touched up her lipstick.

'Better.' Anya nodded and they shared a small smile.

Soon he would hold her, Mika thought longingly as he took up his bow and arrow and went onto the stage.

Anya took a few steps back to position herself for her leap onto the stage.

Roman sat as the performance started.

Out came Ivan the Prince into the enchanted garden.

And Roman waited.

They all did.

Friends who had been through so much waited for this moment and she did not let them down.

As she streaked onto the stage Roman knew the agony behind such gracious, beautiful movements and he respected it.

Just as she would have supported him had he been a boxer.

No, Anya might not have liked it but she would not have held him back and he would do the same for her now.

She was enchanting.

And if she could forgive him about Celeste, Roman thought, then he could sit through this because there was *serious* chemistry on stage.

Anya flirted, no, he corrected himself, Firebird flirted.

And Mika, no, no, Ivan the Prince courted and embraced her and traced her arms, her legs, her spine, with eyes that loved her.

How Mika loved her and as Anya turned she was perfection in his arms and he lifted her high with skilful hands that held her thigh.

Roman cricked his neck.

He was proud, so proud but also relieved when the interval arrived and drinks were very gratefully received.

'I couldn't have done it,' Libby admitted as the women stood and chatted. 'I've always been jealous and wondered whether, if I had pushed myself harder, I could have made it as far as Anya.' She shook her head. 'I couldn't have. Anya is absolutely brilliant and Mika's on fire tonight.'

'He's so hot,' Rachel said.

'He really is,' Naomi agreed.

Daniil gestured with his head to Roman and they pulled slightly aside from the group.

'Are you planning something for Anya?'

They were each other's mirror. They might be a mirror that had broken many years ago but mirrors could break and still they reflected.

'I have a ring,' Roman said. 'I actually had it made at the same time as Nadia's cross. I was just waiting for the right time.'

It was the right time, he was sure.

And it was the right time to be back in his brother's life.

They were back. Roman had never been confirmed the elder, but that was their natural order and he could not have stood to have Daniil looking out for him.

Or Anya.

'Show me.'

'No,' Roman said. 'Because then they'll all come over.'

They went outside and stood beneath the *Firebird* sign and lights, and Roman took the box out of his pocket. Daniil looked at the red stone.

'When I went to have Nadia's cross made I saw this stone. It was pale green then.'

Daniil thought of Anya, all those years ago, peering at him as his cheek was repaired.

Anya had belonged to his brother even then.

It was not pale green now.

It was a deep red.

The stone was Alexandrite.

Discovered in Russia, it was the most elusive and exquisite of stones. It changed colour and was known as Emerald by Day, Ruby by Night.

As was Anya—ice by day, Firebird tonight.

'Are you nervous about asking her?' Daniil asked.

*'Nyet.'* Roman shook his head.

'Liar…'

'I'm not.'

He wasn't.

They headed back inside and Daniil turned and saw Roman bend his head to the side a couple of times as they took the seat.

'You *are* nervous,' Daniil insisted.

'Not about that. I can't stand Mika…' Roman admitted. 'I thought they were just pretty boys in tights.'

Daniil grinned as he realised the cause of his brother's tension as they waited for the second act to start.


Anya was tense too.

She had to be to perform.

She bit into the chocolate treat and sucked in air, and then rolled the foil into a tiny ball.

She was worried about the cleaners throwing it away so it went into the tiny glass case with the feather.

She took a small drink and then touched up her lipstick and headed out.

The orchestra teased and Anya closed her eyes and waited for her time to go on.

The second act was somehow even more amazing. Anya gave it everything that she had.

As she danced she wondered if it were possible to live a dancer's life with Roman by her side. As Ivan lifted her she felt as if she was touching the sky—perhaps she could have it all.

As the egg cracked open Anya felt as if her heart had opened too.

And now she understood why she should dance for herself.

Roman hadn't been working his way back to her, he had worked his way to a better self.

And finally he was here.

The applause was deafening.

And she smiled as she heard him call out to her, 'Bravo, beautiful woman!'

Her eyes searched for him in the darkness but it was then that everything went black. She stood there, momentarily blinded, and closed her eyes.

Then she opened them again, but everything was still black and Anya realised that she was about to faint.

Ivan the prince caught her.

But Roman could only see that Mika swept her into his arms.

The crowd gasped as Tatania dramatically collapsed and was carried from the stage.

The curtain hurriedly came down and a few moments later an announcement was made that Tatania was fine and had suffered a simple faint after giving her all for the audience.

Roman was already backstage by the time the announcement was made and it was more than a simple faint because she lay pale and retching.

The medics were not taking a chance with their star and an ambulance had already been called.

Mika was holding her head and fanning her face and Roman wanted to rip his stupid feather cap off, but he just knelt down and checked for himself how she was.

'I just need to go home and rest,' Anya said.

His was home.

She had fainted after a performance before but tonight she was bundled into an ambulance with an oxygen mask over her face and there was a teeny stand-off between Mika and Roman about who went with her.

'I've got this,' Roman said, and climbed into the back.

Had he, though? Anya thought.

Surely now he would chastise her—would tell her that she needed to take better care of herself, that it had to stop.

'It's okay, baby,' he said, and he took her hand.

They were wheeled into the emergency department and the staff were excited that she had arrived. There were oohs and ahhs over her beautiful costume as Roman dealt with it. He removed her shoes, ballet tights, bandages and make-up, and not once did he tell her off.

The senior doctor came in and they ran some tests and Roman translated.

'What is he saying?' Anya asked.

'They are concerned about the wild chanterelles that you ate last night.'

'You poisoned me,' Anya accused.

'As I pointed out to the doctor, I ate ten times the amount you did and I am fine.'

'Well, you couldn't even catch flu if you tried,' Anya said as the doctor left, 'whereas I have a delicate constitution.'

And Roman smiled.

For that was them.

They knew their dance.

Roman's phone rang and it was Daniil. He said they were all on their way to the hospital and asked how Anya was.

'She will be okay,' Roman said. 'Hold on for a moment...' He went out and asked the doctor if Anya could have hot chocolate and the doctor agreed.

He told his twin of the best café in Paris for hot chocolate and asked him to stop and fetch some for Anya on his way.

Then he went back in to her. 'You look better.'

Roman took down the side of the gurney and she made room with her legs for him to sit on the edge, and still he was not cross.

'There is some colour coming back to your face,' he said.

Panic had hit him as he'd raced backstage, but there in the midst of the pandemonium he'd been glad that he'd been beside her, because with or without him this would still have happened.

She would never have to deal with anything alone again, and for so long she had.

The weight of her mother's expectations, the pressure, the demands of her profession, and he wondered about his decision to leave.

He was still sure that he had been right to do so.

But she no longer had to face the world alone.

And when she was at her very worst he made it her best.

'I've spoiled everything,' Anya said. 'We were all going to go out...'

'We might still,' Roman said, 'just without you.'

And his small smile told her he was joking.

'Or we might just have a little after party here.'

'Some party.' Anya took in a breath. 'I honestly don't know what happened, I felt fine when I was dancing...'

'You were amazing.'

'I think maybe it was just the stress of rehearsals, or maybe...'

And she closed her eyes because she would not change a part of yesterday. It hadn't been the conversation or staying up late or making love that had caused this. She had been tense and teary all week, and yesterday had actually helped things.

'Well, I can't wait any longer,' Roman said.

'Sorry?' Anya frowned.

'I've waited for many years to say this, and I don't want to wait another night.'

He went into his pocket and took out a jewellery box and a faded envelope.

She went for the envelope first and inside it was a letter. She let out several small cries as she read it.

Dearest Anya,
I never wanted to be a burden to you. I know I never said it but I love you.

I have loved you all my life and I still love you in death.

Roman

There were no hearts or kisses, for that was not Roman's way.

'You were never a burden.' And then she found out he would have looked after her even in death.

'I made my will out to leave everything to you. Had I died, Dario or one of my comrades would have seen you got this letter and, if possible, the earring that I carried with me wherever I went.'

And she looked at him as she found out not just that he loved her but that he knew the depth of their love.

'You were by my heart when I jumped out of planes, and you were there with me through war, and when I thought I might die you were with me too.'

He would not have died without her knowing, and that meant more than the world to Anya. She had not been left behind.

'Why didn't you tell me this last night?'

'Last night was to clear the air.'

'And what about at the stage door?' Anya said. 'You should have told me then before I went on.'

'You did not require my love to dance as you did,' Roman said. 'You did that by yourself, for yourself...'

And she understood him some more.

With the drip in the back of her hand and her fingers suddenly shaking, it was Roman who opened the box.

'It's time for us to make it official, Anya. You are my family, always.

'Tomorrow, in sunlight, the stone will be the colour of your eyes. Tonight it is the colour of fire.'

He did not ask her to marry him.

He did not need to ask, he just slid the ring onto her finger and kissed it.

'All the years we wasted,' Anya said with a sob in her voice.

'No. These haven't been wasted years…'

They hadn't been, she realised.

Roman was so proud and so determined in all that he did and he had made his way back to her, and to his twin, only when he had been ready. He had returned proud to reclaim the life he'd had to leave behind.

'What about babies?'

'Anya, I love you. If that's what you want, we can look at other ways.'

'What do you want?'

He had never considered that he might become a father until he had held Nadia.

Then he'd looked at Anya and had never really considered her a mother.

Until now.

Others thought Anya icy, yet he knew her passion and love.

'Yes,' he said. 'Maybe, one day, we could look at adoption. We could go back to Russia…' His voice came the closest it ever had to breaking, because he had never thought he might go back, and certainly never to an orphanage. 'We can work it out.'

They could now.

A nurse popped her head around the curtain and it would seem they had visitors.

'I can tell them to wait,' Roman said. 'Or to go home.'

'I'd like to see them,' Anya said.

She wanted to show them her ring!

And they all spilled in, the men in suits and beautiful, especially Daniil because he was carrying a tray of hot chocolate, and the women were dressed for an evening at the ballet and looked stunning too.

And she could have felt drab, given that she was wearing a hospital gown, but she felt the most beautiful woman in the world as she showed them her ring.

She watched as the twins shook hands and the other men offered congratulations and the women squealed.

'You must come to New York for new year, all of you,' Sev said, and this time Roman didn't roll his eyes.

And Anya would go too. She would because they accepted her. There was no punishment or silent judgment of her predicament tonight.

They seemed to love her as she was.

Their engagement was toasted in hot chocolate that Daniil had bought for everyone.

It was the best after party Anya had ever known.

The medic came back with some equipment and asked everyone to wait outside, but Roman remained.

'He can stay,' Anya said.

The doctor's Russian and English was about as good as Anya's French and so he spoke through Roman.

'He asks how long you have been feeling dizzy,' Roman said.

'Since I ate the mushrooms,' Anya said, and then smiled. 'Just when I came off the stage. I felt sick before but I always do...' She thought of all the work that had gone into the production and all the people who would be disappointed if she couldn't perform. 'Tell him that I have to perform. There are two more nights and a matinée...'

'Let's just find out how you are,' Roman said. 'He's asking when you last had a period.'

She lay back on the pillow and decided that perhaps a translator might have been a better idea because she was about to be told off, and in front of Roman.

'A year…' Anya said, and then gave a small shake of her head as she tried to think. 'Maybe closer to eighteen months. And you can tell the doctor that I don't need a lecture,' she snapped.

Translation was awful. She didn't understand why Roman took twice as long to say her brief words and why he asked questions as the doctor spoke, without translating for her.

She understood why Roman had needed that time to learn English.

It was very disempowering.

'Could you tell me what he's saying?' Anya interrupted Roman in mid-question.

'He says that your electrolytes are fantastic, your iron levels are good, you are supremely fit but that maybe a small lecture might be in order.'

Roman spoke to the doctor again, telling him that Anya did push herself but her diet had been better of late and that no one could do what she did day after day, night after night without being incredibly fit.

And Anya lay there rolling her eyes. It was her consultation and she had not a clue what was being said.

Then she looked at Roman, who had gone very quiet and the hand over hers had tightened.

'What did he say?' Anya asked, and as Roman turned to look at her his face had gone pale and she had the sudden feeling that something was terribly wrong.

'Am I dying?'

'No, Anya.' He started to smile at her drama, but instead he cleared his throat before speaking. 'He said, while he appreciates how fit you are, you are going to need to watch your nutrition for the duration of the pregnancy...'

And the world again seemed to shift, just as it had when she had been on the stage, but it did not go dark. It was as if stars had come out in the sky.

'I can't be pregnant. I haven't...'

What was the point of trying to speak? Roman was asking the doctor questions for her and then answering them as if he knew exactly what she would have asked.

He did.

'You must have ovulated and, instead of getting a period, you fell pregnant,' Roman said. 'He wants to do an ultrasound...'

A nurse rearranged the sheet and Anya lay there with her head spinning and wondering if she dared hope, because even a positive pregnancy test might be wrong.

Except it wasn't.

And they looked at the tiny black circle on the screen and it was her baby and there was a flicker, the beating of a tiny heart.

'He says it is in a nice position,' Roman said, and then he listened as the doctor spoke and was silent for a moment.

'What did he just say?' Anya asked.

'That you are six weeks pregnant and that in a few weeks' time you shall have a more detailed ultrasound, but for now all is fine.'

'I can't be six weeks,' Anya said.

'Anya.' He looked at her. 'It's fine, don't get upset. I know you never expected me to reappear.'

He turned to the doctor and asked a question.

'He said that explains your nausea and dizziness. You can still dance and rehearse...'

But that was not her concern right now.

'Roman,' Anya said, 'tell him that I cannot be six weeks pregnant. You only came back four weeks ago.'

Roman spoke with the doctor again.

'He says that conception would have been four weeks ago. On a usual cycle, it is calculated from the date of your last period.'

Anya lay back stunned and silent and nodded her thanks as the doctor and nurse left them alone.

'He says you can dance tomorrow night and in the future. You are an athlete…' Then he smiled. 'A pregnant firebird, though?'

'Maybe not for long,' Anya said, and she looked at the ring that belonged on her finger and she told him the truth. 'There's been no one since you.'

'Anya, I know about you and Mika…'

She remembered him gritting his jaw at the stage entrance and the hell it must have been for him, watching them dance while thinking that she and Mika were an item, and she knew now just how much Roman loved her.

'No,' Anya said. 'That is just a rumour. I mean it. When I couldn't have you, I gave all I had to my dance.'

And soon they would let the world in. He would tell his twin that he was going to be a father and men who had come so far would congratulate him on the wonderful news, but for now he spoke with the love of his life.

'I will spend the rest of my life making up for the lost years,' Roman said.

'Not lost,' Anya told him. 'Found.'

# EPILOGUE

'SHE'S STILL ASLEEP,' Anya said when she came back onto the balcony, and she could not help but smile at Libby's impatience to meet her new niece.

Daniil, Libby and little Nadia had arrived in Paris early that morning and had been waiting for more than an hour but she was still asleep.

'She was up a few times last night,' Anya explained.

She took a seat and watched as Nadia toddled on little fat legs towards the man she thought was her father, jealous because he was holding a baby. Nadia held out her hands to be picked up then let out a little shocked gasp.

'Wrong one.' Roman smiled at her.

As Nadia toddled off to her real father, Roman looked down at the son he held in his arms.

Dominik.

He was three months old and as Anya looked over she remembered seeing Daniil holding Nadia as a small baby and thinking that this might never happen for them.

It had.

Anya had had to block out the criticism from the press that she was too thin for a woman who was pregnant. And then she'd had the last laugh when she'd given birth to a long-limbed, huge, bonny boy.

Actually, she hadn't laughed at the time, it had hurt an awful lot, but she'd had Roman beside her, telling her she could do it.

And with him beside her, she had.

Seeing Roman hold his newborn in strong arms, the magnitude of that moment would reside in her heart forever.

Oh, he hadn't teared up, this was Roman after all, but, watching him kiss his son and explore his little hands and feet, she'd seen a different side again to a very complex man.

And their dreams had come true in more ways than she had dared hope for.

She was on leave from the dance company but they would be back in Russia in three months' time. They moved between Paris and there with ease, loving both countries and deeply in love.

They had gone to New York and seen in the new year and had had the most wonderful time. All had agreed it would be an annual event.

Yet Roman and Anya had been holding onto a very special secret.

At new year, they had been on their way for their second visit with a little girl who they hoped would one day be their daughter.

Roman's comment about adoption had set their minds thinking and when they'd returned to Russia after *Firebird* had finished to look for a home there, wandering through a magnificent building they had commented about the number of bedrooms and that had led to asking how many babies they wanted.

'If you want more than one, they have to be close,' Anya had said in her own direct way.

She would continue to dance.

Perhaps fewer performances a year but, oh, she would be performing!

'How close?' Roman said. 'It's a shame you're not having twins.'

'I know,' Anya sighed. 'That would have been perfect, two for one…'

And they had stared at each other, neither wanting to be the first to voice it, in case it sounded completely mad.

But they did want more than one child. What they had said before they'd found out that Anya was pregnant had almost felt like a promise to a baby somewhere. The orphanage in Russia where Roman had been raised was gone now but there were many children who needed a home. Anya had felt Roman's tension as they'd stepped inside the *detsky dom*, but it had soon gone.

The sound of laughter had met them and they had glanced inside the dining room.

It had been very different indeed.

And a little the same.

Children had been chatting and there had been jugs of water on the table and some had been lining up for their meals.

The carers here were wonderful and did all they could to make childhood special. Of course, there were problems, yet there was happiness to be found too.

And they had discreetly watched some children playing, unsure how they could possibly choose.

Did they ask about the least wanted one, as Roman had been?

But then she had thought of Daniil, Nikolai, Sev and Roman and how could they ever choose?

You didn't, Anya found out.

Love found you.

She had been three years of age and had very fine blond hair that had stuck up at odd angles. They'd both seen her at the same time, twirling in the playroom and laughing as she did so.

'Tell us about that little one.'

*'Tantsivat...'* The carer had explained that she loved to dance and thought that she was a princess; she fully believed that she was, in fact.

Anya had turned and looked at Roman, who had smiled.

Did they realise that she had Down's syndrome? the carer had checked. 'Most would consider her unsuitable...'

Yes, they did realise she had Down's syndrome, and yet she was so much more than that.

'What is her name?' Roman asked.

'Monica.'

She had been born to be theirs, both knew.

Monica had been the happiest, brightest little girl, she'd just had no family of her own.

Until that moment.

Monica had looked over and had seen the strangers watching and she'd seen that her dancing made the lady smile and so she'd danced a little more.

And then Monica had run over to them, holding out her arms, and Anya had scooped her up; she had simply gathered her into her arms and Monica had smothered her face in kisses.

Leaving her behind had been hell.

They had visited often as they'd waded through the paperwork and the adoption process, and in the midst of it all Dominik had been born.

Last week their family had been made complete.

'Mama! Papa!' Monica's voice came over the intercom.

Monica said it over and over, as she had in the week since she'd been home. She was like a little wind-up doll, practising the words she had always wanted to say.

'I'll go,' Roman said.

But Anya couldn't help herself, and went with him.

And they met Josie at the door, who was running to be the one to greet the little girl too.

She was adored and now knew it.

Monica was sitting up in her pink bed and her blond hair was sticking up as if it had been rubbed with a balloon. Her whole face beamed as they came in and she held out her arms. She was delighted, not just that Mama and Papa had answered her call but that lovely Josie was here and that they'd brought her baby brother in too.

Roman sat on the bed and handed Dominik over.

Anya watched as so very patiently he showed Monica how best to hold him, as his large hands hovered to protect his son.

Dominik looked up at his big sister and smiled at her.

*'Ne plach,'* Monica said, and Anya frowned because Monica was telling the baby not to cry and yet Dominik was smiling.

And then she realised it was Roman who had teared up.

There was so much love in this room, and beyond.

His twin was here, with his wife and niece.

He had all his family safe home.

Roman cleared his throat and then spoke to his daughter. 'We have visitors. Your family have come from England to see you,' he said, and then smiled as Monica reached to her bedside table and put on a little silver plastic tiara.

She was ready now to meet them!

Roman carried both Dominik and Monica with ease and told her that their visitors were her aunt, uncle and a little cousin named Nadia.

'Warn her,' Anya said, remembering Nadia's shocked gasp when she had inadvertently run to Roman instead of Daniil.

'No,' Roman said, smiling.

He knew his little girl.

They walked out onto the balcony and a very happy Monica smiled and gave a royal wave to Libby, who promptly melted on sight.

And then Monica looked at Daniil and her little head cocked to the side and her blue eyes narrowed. Then she turned to look at her papa and then back to Daniil, but then she started to laugh. She had the most infectious laugh in the world.

It was a wonderful day, a family day. After dinner Daniil and Libby jetted back to London with the promise that they would be over to see them very soon.

As Roman put Monica to bed Dominik cried out and Anya went to settle him.

She walked into the cream and lemon room. He lay in the antique crib she had been sure would never be filled, and her heart seemed to squeeze in love for her son.

He would have all the love his father hadn't and Monica would have the same, and she would give her children support rather than obsession.

For whatever they wanted to be.

Just as she'd had Roman's support, in his own unique way.

She opened the door to her dance studio. It had handles up high so that little people would not interrupt her when she trained. Mostly, though, the door was left open and sometimes she exercised with Dominik lying on a mat, kicking his legs in the air as Anya warmed up.

Just this morning Monica had joined her, copying her mother and loving watching herself in the mirror. Roman had suggested that they put in a smaller barre for her.

Anya heard Roman's deep baritone, singing Monica to sleep with the song that still brought tears to Anya's eyes.

She lay on a mat and listened.

Roman had learnt French through song and he was gently teaching Monica the same.

And it was now a song for her.

A little later Roman came in carrying two glasses and two bottles, one of champagne, the other mineral water.

'Hey,' Roman said in surprise when Anya held up her glass for bubbles. 'What's this?'

'You've only ever known me pregnant or nursing, Roman.'

'No,' he said. 'I knew you a long time ago.'

He had.

He filled up her glass and she tasted icy champagne as he joined her on the floor.

There was so much to celebrate and they chinked their glasses but with one sip Anya put hers down.

So too did he.

And as they kissed and made love, as he moved deep within her, she found herself gazing into a mirror.

There were hundreds of images of them, of Anya and Roman.

Yet they made memories now.

\* \* \* \* \*

### #3445 BOUGHT BY HER ITALIAN BOSS
by Dani Collins

Vittorio Donatelli will do anything to protect his company from scandal—he's kept the secret of his true parentage hidden for years. So if it means making stunning Gwyn his mistress to combat the vicious rumors, then he'll do it...with pleasure.

### #3446 THE UNWANTED CONTI BRIDE
*The Legendary Conti Brothers*
by Tara Pammi

If Sophia Rossi wants to save her father's business, then merging the Rossi and Conti empires is the only way. Except Luca Conti broke Sophia's heart once before and can still make her body tremble with just a look!

### #3447 MASTER OF HER INNOCENCE
*Bought by the Brazilian*
by Chantelle Shaw

After it's revealed that Clare Marchant is only disguised as a nun to save her kidnapped sister, Diego suddenly finds himself trading his prize diamond to help her. Now Clare is indebted to the notorious womanizer and he intends to collect...

### #3448 THE FLAW IN RAFFAELE'S REVENGE
by Annie West

Relentless Italian Raffaele Petri needs reclusive researcher Lily Nolan to see his revenge plans come to fruition. But the damaged beauty is feisty, argumentative and all too intriguing to be ignored!

---

The car pulled up at her hotel and Abby wondered if he'd
suggest dinner and if she might accept.

But Matteo, being Matteo, skipped the entrée, main
and dessert and, after such a lovely day, for him the
ending was inevitable.

"We could," Matteo said, "always go to mine."

That delicious mouth moved in for the kill and what
startled Abby the most was that she wanted to accept, to
just close her eyes and give in to the bliss he offered,
except she jerked her head back.

"I'm assuming we're not talking about the restaurant
at your hotel?"

"We're not."

For Matteo, sex was as straightforward and as simple
as that.

"What happened to keeping it strictly business?" Abby
asked.

"I can juggle both."

He looked into green eyes that had been relaxed and smiling all day but now had turned to sleet.

"I'll see you on race day." Abby's voice was tart. He could feel the anger and indignation emanating from her, and Matteo, who only ever played with the willing, leaned back. "If you're still interested, that is." She didn't wait for the driver to open the door for her; instead she got out and slammed it shut.

*You're not here to seduce*, Matteo reminded himself as the driver took his rarely rejected passenger back to his hotel.

Matteo never misread signs.

Today the two of them had blasted a heat to rival a Dubai sun.

It was better this way, he conceded as he climbed out of the car and headed to his luxury suite.

If ever he'd been glad that he hadn't told Abby about the necklace, it was now, because he was seriously interested in the Boucher racing team.

And, far more worryingly for Matteo, he was also seriously interested in Abby herself.

Which was, for a die-hard bachelor, very troubling indeed.

*Don't miss*
***DI SIONE'S INNOCENT CONQUEST***
*by Carol Marinelli,*
*available July 2016 wherever*
*Harlequin Presents® books and ebooks are sold.*

www.Harlequin.com

## HARLEQUIN

# Presents.

*Don't miss the second story in Miranda Lee's*
**Rich, Ruthless and Renowned** *trilogy!*

**The to-do list of a billionaire playboy's secretary:**

1. Filing: ensure all ex-girlfriends are kept safely
   out of sight.
2. Expenses: all jewelry must be received one
   week from termination of relationship.
3. Diary management: there must be no clashes
   in his heavy dating schedule.

When Harriet McKenna's own relationship goes up in smoke,
her ruthless boss, Alex Kotana, challenges her to take a leaf
out of his book and embark on an illicit affair with him! This means
being at his beck and call beyond office hours, but in return
Alex promises to show Harriet how *pleasurable* life can be…

Find out what happens next in

# THE BILLIONAIRE'S RUTHLESS AFFAIR

**July 2016**

**Stay Connected:**
www.Harlequin.com
www.IHeartPresents.com

f /HarlequinBooks

@HarlequinBooks

/HarlequinBooks

HP13448

6786

# JUST CAN'T GET ENOUGH
# OF THE ALPHA MALE?
## Us either!

Come join us at **I Heart Presents** to hear the latest from your favorite Harlequin Presents authors and get special behind-the-scenes secrets of the Presents team!

With access to the latest breaking news and special promotions, **I Heart Presents** is *the* destination for all things Presents. Get up close and personal with the sexy alpha heroes who make your heart beat faster and share your love of these glitzy, glamorous reads with the authors, the editors and fellow Presents fans!